AND THEN THINGS FALL APART

AND THEN THINGS FALL APART

Arlaina Tibensky

Simon Pulse

New York London Toronto Sydney

⋀⋀⋀

SIMON PULSE
An imprint of Simon & Schuster Children's Publishing Division
1230 Avenue of the Americas, New York, NY 10020
First Simon Pulse paperback edition July 2011
Copyright © 2011 by Arlaina Tibensky
All rights reserved, including the right of reproduction in whole
or in part in any form.
SIMON PULSE and colophon are registered
trademarks of Simon & Schuster, Inc.
For information about special discounts for bulk purchases, please contact
Simon & Schuster Special Sales at 1-866-506-1949 or
business@simonandschuster.com.
The Simon & Schuster Speakers Bureau can bring authors to your live event.
For more information or to book an event contact the Simon & Schuster
Speakers Bureau at 1-866-248-3049 or visit our
website at www.simonspeakers.com.
Designed by Karina Granda
The text of this book was set in Caslon.
Manufactured in the United States of America
2 4 6 8 10 9 7 5 3 1
Library of Congress Control Number 2010044631
ISBN 978-1-4424-1323-8
ISBN 978-1-4424-1324-5 (eBook)

For my parents

I once watched a collector kill a monarch butterfly on a nature show by putting it under a glass dome with a piece of cotton soaked in gasoline. The insect's wings flapped less and less until they were perfectly still.

Suffocation is a cruel way to go.

I can't breathe under my bell jar either.

I'm hot.

I have the chills.

I'm drenched with sweat, smothered beneath a hundred-pound coverlet.

My head hurts. My eyes hurt. My tongue feels heavy so it's hard to talk. If I stop typing, a vein in my forehead twitches with my pulse.

I close my eyes, leaning my head back on my pillow to rest. For a second it's as dark as a midnight sky. Then I imagine the shattered pieces of my heart sparkling like mirror shards.

But when I open my eyes, I am still here: in the spare bedroom in my grandma's house with her ancient green bottle of *Muguet des Bois* from her own high school years on the dresser. My deceitful and depraved father is still staying in the basement. My mother is still in California visiting her sister's premature newborn, and my boyfriend, Matt, is still avoiding me.

The best years of my life.

And then the itching resumes with renewed fury.

Because I have the chicken pox. It's a virus that, contrary to popular belief, you can still catch well into your teens.

I think I am losing my mind a tiny bit at a time. When the chatter in my head gets too loud, I start to type. The noise from the typewriter keys drowns out the noise in my head. Getting what I'm thinking onto paper in smudgy black letters feels good, like stretching or punching a wall. Or crying. Which I'm not doing much of anymore because it doesn't seem to help.

I'm not the first person to ever be sick, enraged, depressed, delirious, betrayed, and confused all at the same time, or to use a typewriter to examine life in all of its jagged-edge glory. Sylvia Plath did it too, and she is the most inspired, beautiful, and subversive writer of her generation. She'd be almost one hundred years old if she were alive. So even if she didn't kill herself when she was thirty, she'd be dead by now. At least she left us her poems and <u>The Bell Jar</u>.

<u>The Bell Jar</u> is about a young writer named Esther Greenwood and how she goes a little crazy and then gets better. But the book is really all about how life is unfair. And right now, whose life is more unfair than mine?

It's also about losing your virginity, and babies being alive and beautiful, or dead and grotesque, and either way ruining your life. But mostly it is about how hard it is to be yourself in a world that wants you to be someone who is easier to deal with. And it's about writing. Which I also love. And trying to kill yourself, which I'm so not into, even though being alive is sofa king hard for me lately.

For the past four months I've been reading my tattered dog-eared copy of the novel over and over again because it seems like the sanest thing to do. The book is challenging and comforting and often hilarious, unlike my own day-to-day, which is none of those things. Sylvia Plath is there for me when actual living people upon whom I have depended my whole life, are not. What I mean to say is, without her words, I'd be exponentially more messed up than I am already.

Do I have a computer? A link to the outside world? No. My cell is even out of commission since the last fight I had with Matt when I flung it against the wall of the walk-in freezer at my parents' restaurant. The screen's not cracked or anything, but the # key chipped off and is somewhere in a vat of shredded mozzarella. I didn't tell my parents, because then they would have asked what the fight was about. (My virginity! Huzzah!) And for all I know, some poor customer is going to swallow a # key and die of a ruptured intestine and sue my parents, and it will all be my fault.

Without real entertainment, I will try anything to amuse myself. Not unlike the polar bears at the Brookfield Zoo, I need complex toys to keep me from going insane in my ten-by-ten cage. When Gram lugged this electric typewriter up from the basement this morning so I could practice my "typing skills," I was actually excited. She gave me a lesson on shifting and carriage return before she left to drop off shirts for my dad at the dry cleaner's.

It's a gray-green IBM, and weighs about a thousand pounds, but actually it is pretty amazing. Fast. When I hit the keys, they *clickity-clack*. As the ink presses onto the paper, it's like I'm actually making something. Like art.

Maybe it's the pox, or my frying brain, but all I really want to do is type. I'm sick of being a hunt-and-pecker, typing like an intelligent duck. I was halfheartedly taking an online keyboarding class, and would have still been at it if I hadn't gotten stricken in my prime. But I am trapped in this little bedroom, which used to be my great-grandma's before she died. I'm alone with this antique typing device. My brain. And a fever. How much more Plathian can I be?

Computers are quiet and clean and totally distracting because the Internet is there, lying in wait for a moment of weakness to pounce on your creativity and progress. Sylvia didn't have to deal with Facebook. Blogs. Etsy. Twitter, for Christ's sake.

Gram just has basic cable, so TV is rather limited, but doable. The woman makes perfect boiled eggs, though, and buys the really good orange juice, the Sabor Latino with guava kind that my mom says smells like feet. Weird, the things that are making me miss my mom. She's in Los Angeles, but she might as well be in Siberia.

My head is throbbing and I am scratching so much that the sheets are leopard printed with spots of light pink blood. Not that my father would even notice. Dad is either working alone at the restaurant or driving the Dine & Dash delivery van around the streets of his youth, wondering where the hell it all went wrong and thinking not at all about his abandoned, ailing, and itchy only child—me.

FLEABITES

High on the exam table,

You watch me from the doorway.

While the doctor twists my arm

This way

And that.

A specimen.

My heart plays dress-up.

Disguised as a little girl,

I am asleep on a merry-go-round.

Itching and aching,

Mouth dry as toast.

What to do?

Daddy, Daddy, you traitor, I'm through.

DATE: July 13
MOOD: Dickensian
BODY TEMP: 101.6

If you get the chicken pox the summer before your sophomore year of high school, it is your parents' fault. They—
i.e., your parents—are supposed to get you booster shots.
Tetanus. Whooping cough. Chicken pox. MMR (measles,
mumps, rubella—whatever that last one is). This is totally
routine parenting, people. In fifth grade the school secretary
even sent home notes. Notes. To the home! An eight-year-old
would have taken better care of a doll than my parents did of
me, then—now. Whatev.

Pox. Sounds like a Japanese candy, but alas, they are
tiny, little blisters that the first doctor my father begrudg-
ingly dragged me to diagnosed as—are you sitting down?—
fleabites. FLEA. BITES. Because there was no way this
doctor could believe that the alluring, practically adult young
woman standing before him in a paper exam smock could
have the most anecdotal of childhood diseases.

"Do you have a dog?" The doctor asked my father.

Neither of us knew where he was going with this. I mean we do/did have a dog, Coffee, who is staying at my grandma's house—Mom's mom's, not Dad's mom's, which is where we are staying now. So!?

We nodded slowly like we were negotiating with a mugger.

"Does it have fleas?" he asked. Have I mentioned that I had a 130-degree temperature? That I was running around town without eyeliner? That I was wearing whatever had been on top of my pile of dirty laundry, and until I had looked down at my body on the way into the doctor's office, I hadn't even known what I put on?

"You see"—the doctor used a pen as a pointer to indicate a pox on my forearm—"there is a center depression where the proboscis entered. And this tiny cluster of blisters surrounding it? A severe allergic reaction." He actually used the word "proboscis" like he was an SAT tutor.

As I was trying to get my (dirty) hoodie zipped back up so me and my fleabites could just get home—I mean, to Gram's—my dad did something I have not seen him do, not once in the past three months since Mom kicked him out of the house. He acted like—a man. Not just a biological man, but like Indiana Jones or Kiefer Sutherland. At first I thought he was going to punch Dr. Proboscis's lights out. Instead Dad poked the quack in the chest and said, "My daughter doesn't have fleas, idiot. Go to hell."

Then he dragged me out the door and into the delivery van.

Swearing is another thing I've never heard him do, really. "Go to hell!" is about as R-rated as my dad gets. He was worried about me, I guess. Probably worried about everything. And by everything I mean every possible thing that he could be worried about in every aspect of his life—marriage, business, self-esteem, STDs, fathering skills, etc.

My parents own this restaurant together called the Dine & Dash. The ampersand (&)—yes, I learned this in keyboarding class—is included in the name. They serve all the typical Chicago crap that tourists can't get enough of—Italian beef sandwiches, "Chicago-style" hot dogs (is there any other style?), fries, fruit punch from a fountain, deep-dish pizza. As I sat in the delivery van, with my face on fire with pox fever, my dad drove like such a maniac that boxes of cups and lids from Sam's Club slid back and forth on the floor behind our seats; I thought I was going to hurl.

"Wait until we get to the clinic before you get sick, Keek, okay? Crack the window. Try not to think about the giant bags of pepperoni in the back of the van." This made Dad laugh—not a cruel ha-ha but a little we're-in-this-together chuckle. I was so sick that I didn't think how cool it was to hear him laugh until later that night under the hundred-pound coverlet my grandma insisted on using to smother me with—even though it's July.

At the clinic, of course, my chicken pox was correctly identified. I didn't even have to take my clothes off and put on the paper dress. The receptionist basically diagnosed me on the spot. About three weeks of fluids and bed rest, the doctor said. It's like the flu, but with infectious and hideous wounds that itch like fire-breathing ants all over your body and could scar you for life if treated improperly.

My dad wrote the clinic a check.

The doctor told me that everything was going to be fine and patted me on the head. But he didn't know the half of it. I wasn't about to fill him in on all the gory details. That my mom had kicked my dad out of the house for sleeping with a waitress who was, for lack of a better term, my best friend. That instead of moving into his own apartment or at least the YMCA like divorcing men do on sitcoms, my dad had moved into the basement apartment of his mother's house. We also didn't mention that my aunt had just given birth to a baby almost three months early that weighed three pounds and ten ounces, and that Mom went to stay with her for a few weeks, or until the baby died, whichever came first. I didn't tell them that two weeks of bed rest would totally derail my summer learning program—that is, basic keyboarding and rereading The Bell Jar for the ninth time—or that staying in my grandmother's house miles away from my boyfriend, friends, and dog, with my dad crying himself to sleep in the basement every night, might just possibly make me want to shove my head into an oven.

Matt.

When I am into him, I love his name because it is short and strong, like he is. A perfect name for a varsity wrestler, which he is. When I hate him, I also hate his name. Matt, like a doormat or a sweaty wrestling mat or a ball of matted hair in the shower drain. Matt, short for Matthew. But who calls him Matthew? No one but his mother when she's mad at him.

My hair was brown and long when we started going out. My parents lived in the same house and slept in the same bedroom, down the hall from my own. Back then Matt and I would walk to the Dine & Dash, and Amanda would serve us free Cokes and fries, and then we'd walk to his house and make out insanely until his/my hormones started to freak me out and/or my mouth got all raw.

We also went on dates, lots of them, sometimes in groups and sometimes just us. And we laughed. All the time, at anything we wanted to, because everything seemed hilarious to us. We were a textbook example of the happiest high school couple on earth.

And then my parents started to fight by not talking to each other. I dyed my hair black. And bleached parts of it, dyeing those parts pink. And then Free-Fry Amanda became That-Stupid-Slut-That-Ruined-Everything Amanda. And I started to write poetry on my tights with black Sharpie marker and wear them to school beneath vintage thrift store pencil skirts.

Then the wrestling team went to nationals, and Matt started hanging out more with the other wrestlers, and one of them had a blond sister, a freshman with an A name. Amy? Anne? Jennifer? Whatever the hell her name was, she wore Keds with no retro irony whatsoever, and I know she was crushing on Matt because she would look right past me—his *girlfriend*—whenever we passed each other in the hall. Maybe she was scared. Afraid to look the crazy girl in the eye. And I'm sure she was totally—what is the word?—*incredulous* that Matt in all his mainstream hotness would have anything to do with a mess in scribble tights and hair from hell.

Matt still came over, but we talked a lot less and kissed a lot more, and I started to think that maybe we were in love. I mean, I was. Like mature and sophisticated love where you share feelings and really communicate and grow, and whatever else people are supposed to do in a "relationship."

And that's when all the *sex pressure* began. Lately, especially, it's been like, "Hi, Keek. Did you get the algebra notes? Oh, and can I put my penis inside you, just a little bit?"

Okay. Not quite that ridiculous, but the boy is—and let's face it, I too am—slightly obsessed. When I'm on my deathbed and the great moments of my life flash before my eyes, I want the Great Virginity Losing to be right up there with winning the Pulitzer. Argh. Sex. It's all we seem to talk about and think about—doing it, not doing it.

It's supposed to be no big deal. According to CNN and concerned parenting websites, twelve- and thirteen-year-old girls are supposedly having tons of sex all over the place. Virginity is so Jane Austen. It is so Zeus disguised as a swan deflowering pale damsels by mountain streams in Greece. It is what chivalrous knights of King Arthur's court jousted to the death to protect. Basically, it is an ancient, epic, powerful force, and more important to me than I let on.

I know for sure what sexy is—or what shampoo commercials, men's razor blade ads, Victoria's freaking Secret, and *Maxim* magazine want me to think is sexy. Yes, I know it so well, I could pull together a PowerPoint presentation about it for virgins everywhere.

And I can *be* that kind of sexy, whether or not I think it is really, truly, and authentically sexy—like, to me. How easy is it to put on a push-up bra, crawl on all fours, and lick someone's neck? A child could do it!

But what do I myself find sexy? What do I feel sexy doing, regardless of what I'm *supposed* to think is sexy? Dear reader, I am still figuring it the hell out.

For instance, when Matt sprayed himself with some kind of musk oil and pressed his face into mine, smelling like a rotting mink carcass, I did not find that sexy. But. Slow dancing with him while he whispered the song lyrics into my ear? Hot. I also like a little neck biting. Textbook vampire crap, I know, but still. I love lying down together and trying to take a nap and not being able to. And what I love so much about Matt is that he wants to let me figure it out with him. He doesn't seem to mind that he is my guinea pig. I wish it was the same for him.

Only a week ago Matt and I having our very first times together was the most important goal in my life. I savored every moment we were alone because I knew that one day we would finally crash our bodies together all the way and it would be an Armageddon of amazingness. And we would reach such levels of togetherness that the angels would weep with jealousy. Only a week ago.

But since our fight in the freezer, I haven't seen or talked to Matt, which is a record for us. I have the chicken pox. I am at my grandma's house. My parents are a mess. The last thing I want to think about is Matt. Except, because of everything, I can't seem to help it.

Besides Matt, there aren't many people who would

care to know where I am. I've been a little wrapped up in myself lately. I mean, when I say I am under a bell jar same as my comrade in depression, Esther Greenwood, I am not kidding. It's hard to breathe in here. Thoughts bounce around the inside of my head like Ping-Pong balls in a see-through vacuum cleaner. Bounce, twist, bounce, twist, and then they all collide in midair and I am, suddenly, no fun to be around. I'm so busy listening to myself droning on and on in the echo chamber that, believe me, I'm not calling up my old pal Nicola to chitchat and work on our upcycled Etsy shop. I'm barely washing my hair. Like Esther, I'm feeling like, What's the point? It's just going to get dirty again. Which is, I'm sure, how a perfectly sane person begins to slowly go crazy until two months later she is finger-weaving macramé belts from used dental floss instead of updating her Facebook status, eating food, or getting out of bed.

When my fever is at its highest—or today, anyway—I see tiny letters, like *a, s, d, f, g, j, k, l,* flapping like butterflies in front of my face. The letters are all different colors.

Matt is very beautiful. His whole body is taut, and his muscles are watery like the frog we dissected in biology. Which sounds entirely psychotic, like my boyfriend's a mutant frogboy, which is not what I mean. I mean he is very fluid and stronger than he looks. I once watched him pin this ridiculously solid senior in thirty seconds. We wrestle, but he always lets me win. And let me tell you, I am a mess over him.

But how will he even know that I am not dead? Last time we talked, we had this fight, and I acted like I was okay with everything when I wasn't, really. Instead of screaming at him and weeping and whatever else I probably should have done, all I said was that I had a really bad headache and that I had to go home and that maybe I'd see him later.

Later became Mom getting the phone call from Auntie and jetting off to California, and then me and the Dr. Proboscis fiasco, and me staying at my grandma's in the upstairs bedroom while my father lurks in the basement like a caged monster. And the only available phone is harvest-wheat colored with square push buttons and is down the hall. Gram should sell it for big money on eBay as a freaking retro collectible.

There used to be furniture made especially for telephones. Telephone chairs and telephone tables. Which is so sad, seeing as how there are no more phones like that. I mean, besides Gram, how many people still have a landline?

My mom told me that when she was a little kid, the phone company set up this number where you could call Santa before Christmas. A recording would answer "Ho, ho, ho!" and then talk about some Christmas tradition from Holland (straw for the reindeer in the shoes) or the Czech Republic (walnuts or chocolate coins in stockings). Mom called the Santa line five times a day until she got in trouble for running up the phone bill.

She also told me that you could call a number and they would tell you what time it was. WHY? Today all you have to do is look at your cell phone, which is calibrated to the correct time via satellite in outer-freaking-space. Whatev. No one's calling me on any device of any kind, retro, broken, satellite-calibrated, or otherwise.

I think I am hallucinating. Before the letter *Q* crash-landed on my left thumb knuckle, it flapped around and looked like this:

Q   Q

                         Q

                         Q

Q

                                     Q

                         Q

Q

                                               Q

Q   Q

                       Q

                       Q

Q

Time to sleep.
ZZZZZZZZZZZZZZZZZZZZZZZZZZZZZZZZZZZ
ZZZZZZZZZZZZZZZZZZZZZZZZZZZZZZZZZZZ
ZZZZZZZZZZZZZZZZZZZZZZZZZZZZZZZZZZZ
ZZZZZZZZZZZZZZZZZZZZZZZZZZZZ

DATE: July 15
MOOD: All by Myself I Am a Huge Camellia
BODY TEMP: 103.5

Sylvia actually wrote a poem called "Fever 103°" that's in her other masterpiece, a book of poems called <u>Ariel</u>. The poem is all about flushing and heat and going and coming and giant flowers, and I always thought it was about, er, sex. Oh, dear reader, a true Plathian cannot survive on <u>The Bell Jar</u> alone.

Fever and sex are totally similar, I guess. I'm starting to think all poetry is, in an oblique and cunning way, about human desire and copulation. Even that Carl Sandburg poem "Fog" that we all had to memorize in fourth grade:

> The fog comes
> on little cat feet.
> It sits looking
> over harbor and city
> on silent haunches
> and then moves on.

Could be about sex if you think about fog as desire and the city as a teenager.

Maybe it's just me.

Chicken pox, by the way, are really vile. And itch. Christ, do they itch. I'm a mature and sophisticated teenager, and I can barely stop scratching. I want to scratch as badly as I imagine addicts crave heroin. I will scratch until my skin bleeds. I will throw a sheet over the itchiest part of my body and rub through the cotton until a little watery blood seeps through, and then, for good measure, just to show the pox who is boss, I scratch some more.

But not my face. Little kids don't know not to scratch their face, so I guess I'm ahead of the game there. Not that I'm so gorgeous or anything, but I'm not ugly, either. And yet I am still avoiding my reflection in the mirror because the pox, when the light is a certain way, look exactly like Big Tim's acne in algebra and seeing that—on my own face!—is so depressing, it might just push me over the edge. The edge of what, I don't know, but every day I feel like I'm clawing my way back to stable ground but can't quite make it to safety. Like can't . . . hold . . . on . . . much . . . longer . . . But of course, I do. Dad does. Mom does. What is the freaking alternative?

Mom didn't even call to let me/us know her plane got in okay. My phone is a piece of scrap metal, right? And I suppose she didn't want to call the house and have to talk to her soon-to-be ex-mother-in-law.

I, too, am avoiding my grandma, which is hard when you are bedridden and she is the one home all day taking care of you. I'm embarrassed in front of her, like what my dad did has something to do with me. You think I'm upset about my father's ridiculous behavior with Amanda and the way he royally broke my mom's heart and totally screwed up my life, and demolished our entire family? Believe me, my grandma is not feeling like mother of the year. I can just imagine a bumper sticker on her Saturn, PROUD PARENT OF A MIDLIFE ADULTERER! She makes hard-boiled eggs for me to snack on and walks around the house smoking Winstons. When she leans over to plump my pillows, she smells like the back room at the restaurant where the dishwashers have their smoke breaks in winter. And instead of gagging, I inhale more because it smells like things used to be, before the shit hit the fan. My life. Right now.

Oh, and it's summer and ninety-seven degrees, but my teeth are chattering nonstop.

My mother raised me to think all men are kind of stupid. Albert Einstein wasn't stupid, but he also wasn't so nice to his wife and could barely dress himself in the morning. My father can run a business, but he barely remembers to put gas into the van.

To be fair, males and females are practically different

species entirely. In high school the boys run around like eighth graders hopped up on Fruity Pebbles, and the girls already know about Kegel exercises, existentialism, and the three *C*s of diamond valuation (color, cut, and clarity). Even now, in my soon-to-be sophomore year there are some boys who still don't shave. Or smell when they sweat. Or realize that girls do not have cooties. How the hell are these poor simps supposed to know how to sweep a girl off her feet or unburden her of her pesky virginity with the painless dashing aplomb of a dark-eyed, stubbled movie star?

I'm not sure what I'm talking about here. All I know is that Matt is not dumb. He is also no Einstein. But he's just like Einstein. He knows how to spread his fingers apart on my back when we lie down, his mouth on my mouth until I can see how in love we are with my eyes closed. He refers to Sylvia Plath as "that friend of yours," and I'm not sure if he is kidding or if he really thinks we borrow each other's clothes and have sleepovers. He knows how to make a night out in the city—to see a band or eat sushi or whatever—fun and safe and dangerous, and still get me home on time. But he doesn't understand how I could want to stay home by myself once in a while.

"What do you do? Like, watch TV and stuff?" We have been together for more than a year. I read. Duh. I write poetry and make bracelets and earrings from nonrecyclable kitchen items. I take pictures with my digital camera of things underwater and make note cards out of them on Snapfish.com. I teach myself how to do actual DIY things from the Internet, like knit, make crepe paper roses, and soap with olive oil. Sometimes I just cram my earbuds into my ears, listen to Beethoven for an hour and a half, and stare out the window at the baseball diamond across the street and think.

He—and when I say "he," I could mean any guy in high school—is very body identified. Matt especially needs to keep his body active and exercised, like a Labrador puppy. As long as his body is involved—eating, making out, running, wrestling, driving, etc.—he seems to know how to behave. When it's just us talking, especially on the phone and there are no bodies to distract him, he can't quite keep up his end of the conversation. He knows enough at the end to say "I love you," but after "Hi, Keekie" and before the love declaration, there are a lot of ums, ohs, and I dunnos.

It's not that I think he's dumb. I don't. He's not. Matt starts AP History in the fall. It's just that right now his body is doing all the thinking. I like him. I like his body. So there's not really much of a problem. And sometimes he really does get me, like he is absorbing more of me than he lets on, and when I need it, he lets me know. And it makes up for all the other stuff that doesn't fit so great, and I think about doing it with him all over again. But then again, he is smart enough to withhold vital information from the love of his life. And I thought that was me.

For someone who loves to be alone a lot, I'm start-ing to go a little crazy. No one is really talking with me, to me, around me. Since I started hanging out so much with Matt, and frittering the rest of my time away with the backstabber-to-the-stars Amanda, I have been totally ignor-ing my friend Nicola—aka, Nic. And what I mean is, almost entirely. She just doesn't get it. It takes too many words to explain the details of what's happening with me to her, a girl I have known since grade school, who gets straight *A*s, who never says "fuck" in front of adults, who doesn't have her virginity hanging on by a thread. She has probably written me off. Which I deserve, I suppose.

So, yeah, lots of silence except for the occasional dog bark and ice-cream truck jingle. And like Esther Greenwood, I find the silences—the world's and my own—are totally depressing me. I'm not exactly initiating conversations here. I'm asleep most of the time, and then I wake up and want to cry and scratch at the same time, which is confusing.

Crying and scratching. They are both supposed to offer relief, but they don't. My muscles feel bruised and my bones hurt where they get near my skin. I am happiest when I'm typing. And then I push the typewriter off my lap and curl my body around it like a sea horse and fall asleep like Esther, knowing that when I wake up, things will be more or less exactly the same.

ANAGRAMS FOR THE TIME BEING

In a bell jar everything is

Distorted.

Words lose meaning but gain momentum.

Amanda, friend from hell,

Becomes a

Half-informed alderman.

Sylvia Plath

Is

Lavishly apt.

Mother, Father, Amanda, and me

Almost transforms into the

Madmen of the Earth Armada.

This one reluctant virgin

Is now an

Earth-convulsing nitrite.

Jesters gesture,

And

Listen

Now is

Silent.

DATE: July 16
MOOD: Limp As a Wet Leaf
BODY TEMP: 103.5

In <u>The Bell Jar</u> Esther gets ptomaine poisoning from bad crabmeat on the *Ladies' Day* banquet table. She's in the bathroom puking her guts out, all shivery and pummeled by tsunamis of nausea. Which is totally how I felt today as I retched into the toilet. And I mean *exactly.* I am utterly and completely as sick as I have ever been.

Well, once I had a stomachache so bad, my parents finally dragged me to a pediatrician, who thought I might have appendicitis and so did a rectal exam—yes, a RECTAL exam—only to determine that I had a stomach flu.

My parents have their own business, and health insurance costs a freaking fortune. We have it, but visits at the peak of illness before I die are cheaper in the long run than shucking out cash for regular checkups when I am apparently healthy. Thank you, Dine & Dash, for making my life even more miserable than it is already.

In Sylvia Plath's masterpiece, <u>The Bell Jar</u>, the modern classic beloved by passionate, sophisticated girls the world over, Esther Greenwood returns to her mother's suburban home after a whirlwind trip to NYC, where she sort of lost her mind. She is demoralized by being alive. She is home-sick for something she has never experienced. She longs for something she cannot explain while dogs yap behind fences and station wagons roll down quiet blacktopped streets. It freaks her out and inspires her to down a jar of sleeping pills.

Being at Gram's isn't as bad as all that, but it ain't so spectacular either. Gram has this neighbor, June, who has a brown Labrador named Hershey, like the chocolate, who wants to maul all humans. I like animals. I am kind of into them, seeing as how they are becoming extinct left and right—practically keeling over and dropping dead all around the world. Even my pseudo-vegetarianism is a non-cruelty thing. Kind of like how the Hippocratic oath works for doc-tors: First, do no harm. I try, unlike most of the adults I have the misfortune to know, not to hurt people and/or animals. At least not on purpose. So if eating a peanut butter and jelly sandwich means one less horrifically slaughtered long-lashed cow, why not? Is meat really so delicious?

And so this dopey dog, Hershey, barks and snarls and bares his teeth at anything that walks on two legs. That includes mail carriers, Gram, me, garbage men, babies, kids on bikes. I have often sat, chin in hand, daydreaming of Amanda reaching down to pet Hershey, saying, in that stupid Betty Boop voice she liked to put on for effect, "Ooh, what a nice wittle doggy," right before Hershey lunges three feet into the air and chomps on the side of her face, skewering her eyeball with his canines.

His bark is not chocolaty. It is like this: *Woowoo! Woowoo! Woo! Snarl, snarl. Woowoo Woowoo! Woo!* And then he slam dances against the chain-link fence until June lets him back inside the house. Every two hours, the Hershey show. *Woo!*

I totally relate to Hershey. He is cute and ferocious. He's as trapped as the rest of us here. Maybe he was hurt before, or is, like, a rescue dog or something. Abused. Because when you have been hurt, and I mean betrayed, and your heart gets tromped on by people you really trusted and loved, you get kind of mean. And skittish. At least for a while.

Speaking of betrayal, let us not forget the boyfriend who has forsaken me; or my beloved and adulterous father hiding in his lair in the basement—so depressed and self-centered, I can hardly look at him when he emerges; or my fever and itching and overall malaise. Or that my mom has pretty much abandoned me. And no, it's not suicide-inducing, but it is pretty strenuous on my coping skills.

The icing on the cake is that I am having some kind of technology withdrawal. I'm here all alone and it's not horrible, but it is *quiet*. Silent. There's no radio music, no TV blaring in the next room. No street noise slipping in through the open windows. And the loneliness is like an invisible animal in the room, like a giant cat. Every once in a while I feel like I could stretch my arm out past the typewriter on the bed, touch its tail, place my palm on its enormous flat head, and stroke its ears.

Without the Internet I feel unplugged from the world. There is a new stillness that I have never noticed before. With computers you can set up your whole day so that everyone you have ever known or want to know is sitting in one big cyber room, waiting for you to show up. Whether you do or not, they are there. And knowing they are there is a great comfort. And it's not just the cyber room but the entire world at your fingertips. The *globe* is your freaking oyster. Without it, here, under the covers, my world is—this room. This bed. This brain. All my annoying and heartbreaking problems. And an invisible cat curled up on the pillow next to my head, waiting for me to pass out so it can smother me while I sleep.

The nurse at the clinic warned me. When you get chicken pox at the recommended age of six, seven, or eight, it lasts about three days. If you are about nine or ten, it's perhaps four to five days of light fever and slight pox, and then, alley-oop it's all over before the week is out. When, however, you are fifteen and contract the chicken pox (I so wish I could Google "chicken pox" and share its Latin name and other fancy-pants knowledge about my illness, but, oh, that's right, I'm in a computer-free information ABYSS), you get very—and I mean extremely—sick. It is worse than worse. It is akin to getting the bubonic plague or smallpox like they show on PBS documentaries.

I have moments of great strength in which I drag the typewriter onto my bedridden lap and type away. These moments are immediately followed by moments of great weakness and existential ennui, after which I basically pass out for a few hours.

Woo, woo! Snarl, snarl.

Lather. Rinse. Repeat.

MEAT AISLE

My heart is sliced into pieces,
As red and glistening as marbled steaks
Wrapped in cellophane.
A sorrowing beast,
Its timid snout protrudes,
Sniffing and panting,
Hot breath and whiskers.
I am howling.
My teeth itch to snatch at skins.
My arms ache to embrace.
My essentials long for trust, security,
A safe bed in front of the fire,
Where I can rest before tomorrow's hunt.

DATE: July 17
MOOD: The Opposite of Hopeful
BODY TEMP: 101

I just had a dream about my aunt's baby. An invisible giant cat weighs more than it does. In the dream the baby had gigantic golden eyes like Gollum from *The Lord of the Rings* movie. And it was covered in blood and floating in a Sam's Club–size mayonnaise jar in my grandma's fridge—just like the pickled fetuses Esther stares at in <u>The Bell Jar</u>.

I don't know what's going on with the baby. I don't even know if it's a boy or girl or if they've given it a name, whatever it is. I'm assuming it's a girl and I'm assuming that she will die. What I am projecting on this poor creature is hopefully a thousand times worse than what is really happening. Lightbulb-shaped skull. Holes in the heart. Undeveloped lungs, and gills.

I have a good fifteen years on this infant in California. Unlike Esther Greenwood, I have not seen a woman giving birth in real life. We watched a DVD in health class. I think it was supposed to scare us to death from having sex—as in,

"Beware! This could happen to you, and by you I mean you specifically, Keek. So let this be your warning. *Do not do it with that wrestler.*"

But I am not a squeamish person. I also like to think that I am, in my own suburban way, a little fearless. Just like Esther Greenwood, I like to stare at people and things in dire and horrible circumstances, like homeless amputees on Michigan Avenue and bloody accidents on the expressway. I dare myself to pry my eyelids apart and take it all in, staring so hard the images and feelings burn into my soul forever. And so it was with this DVD in the classroom with half the shades drawn and the volume turned up high enough to drown out snide remarks from the stupid boys.

We sat there watching a woman with no makeup walking around a hospital room and breathing like she was doing some kind of experimental yoga. Her husband/lover had a ponytail and beard. (How old was this footage?) Then jump cut to the woman on her back with her knees up at her ears, and there's this total, like, crotch shot, but it was so not arousing to anyone.

At first I didn't even know what I was looking at, and I, um, have one. There was what looked like a wall of hair, and Matt's best friend, Earl the Squirrel, guffawed and said, "Wax much?" Hardee har har.

Then there was pushing on the mom's part and the

husband/lover in the room saying, "Come on, honey. You can do it. I love you, here it comes," etc. The mom was working so hard, her lips were bared back from her teeth like a cantering horse, and she was biting down and frowning like she was casting a spell. And then this little hairy head stretched her apart, and then a little squished-up face, and then *sploosh!*

It looked just like Esther said: kind of bluish and powdered with white, like a plum dipped in flour. And my jaw was on the freaking floor and my heart was racing up into my ears, and it was as if the whole world held its breath for one full minute.

The baby looked like it was covered in wax, and it squalled like a baby animal. It had a courageous little penis like a little purple chocolate, and they wiped him off and wrapped him in a white blanket with blue and pink stripes. First there was nothing, and then there was this beautiful and adorable baby blinking at the camera.

And this is where we all come from.

The magnificence of it made me suddenly feel old. When I looked around the room, most kids were staring down at their textbooks or scratching imaginary itches, but to my utter shock and surprise there was Earl the Squirrel, wet-faced with tears like my mom at a wedding.

All I could think of was Matt, how he would have liked to have seen this too, how I would have liked to have seen it with him. It's not like I'm going to Netflix educational DVDs about the birthing process to watch while eating popcorn and microwaved bean burritos, but I thought about birth and birthing and babies and the freaking meaning of life for almost a month straight. Matt tried to understand, but really, he didn't see the video, did he? He had no idea what I was talking about.

Esther's boyfriend, Buddy (his real name!), shows her (a) an actual woman giving birth and (b) a bunch of fetuses in jars of formaldehyde. Which, I think, is why my brain went there in the first place. When it comes to the baby-having, I don't really think about it much. As it pertains to me. I mean, I'm fifteen. Babies are something I assume I will have one day, like my driver's license, a college degree from a decent school, my own apartment in the city. Marriage is for the birds, from what I've seen of it. Maybe I'll change my mind, but thanks to Marriage with a capital *M*, I'm all kinds of sad today. Marriage seems to suck, but babies are all right. Kids are even better. I was a flower girl at my aunt's wedding, and now her baby is on infant life support.

In movies when there is a dog, I always kind of brace myself for the moment when the dog will eat poison, get shot, get run over, drown, etc. And then when the dog dies (they always do; that is their function in the film, to die), I weep and basically lose my mind over it. And that is for make-believe dogs on the silver screen. How must it feel to lose an actual baby?

Baby birds, when they fall out of their nests in the spring, are bluish with skinny necks and translucent eyelashes. What is life, anyway? Is the baby aware of what's going on? How dire the situation is? Is it in pain? What could it possibly be thinking of? Is it just mute and senseless, waiting for people to touch it, writhing under Plexiglas? That's its life? This baby and I share so much DNA that if it needed a kidney, we would probably be a perfect match, being cousins and all.

These musings were all—what's the word?—*academic* before I watched the stupid Pampers, Downy, and Johnson & Johnson baby shampoo commercials. Oh, daytime TV. I mean, it was so very sad when Old Yeller died. But he wasn't *actually* my dog. And it was also sad about the early birth, but it was hard to think of the baby as *actually* my cousin. But then I was lying here, scratching and not really paying attention, until there was the most amazing parade of adorableness that American advertising has to offer. Babies—what seemed like hundreds of them—sleeping, cooing, dimpling, making cute baby food messes. Learning how to walk. Being licked into hysterics by wiggling golden retriever puppies. Clapping their little chubby hands together, innocent and loving and alive with joy the way only babies can be.

And our baby became flesh-and-blood real to me for the first time. Whatever they need to save you, a lung, a chunk of my liver, my pancreas—take it all. I don't need it as badly as you do. I'm so tired of being the only child in my family, my limbs ache from it. She deserves the chance to be bowled over by a puppy. This baby is all potential. I love her sofa king much already. Whether she makes it or not.

I want to be able to look back on this time of my life and laugh or even just smirk a little. I want to look back like in a rearview mirror at this horrible bloody smash-up of a summer. I want to live through this and move on, and if my little cousin can just hang in there and stick around long enough to have a life, all this crap my family is going through will seem inconsequential. Why couldn't this one baby, our little baby, splash out in textbook fashion like the one I saw in health class? Who decides what is fair? WTF?

Although I can't stop imagining my cousin trapped in a giant mayonnaise jar, I still love mayonnaise. It is one of my favorite things ever. The King of Condiments. Up yours, Ketchup. Esther felt the same way about caviar. I've only had the kind of caviar that comes in tiny decorative jars in the pickle aisle of the grocery store, but maybe the expensive stuff is better. Despite my feelings on the matter, Esther is a fool for caviar and spreads it as thickly as peanut butter on anything she can get her hands on.

In the same way, I could eat mayonnaise like ice cream—and have, at the restaurant. From the giant jar. Just one massive *clean* (I am always Illinois health code compliant) spoonful, and then I screw the lid back on and go back to the phones to take delivery orders. Who would ever know that I do this? And who would care? How many times did I just take a second to feed my need when we were totally swamped, and no one was the freaking wiser? My eating mayo on the sly is not even in the same league as you sleeping with the waitress at your establishment just because you can and because you think no one will ever find out, Dad. Sofa king different, it's not even funny.

This is all I have to think about. This and this and THIS. Matt. Baby. Mother. Father. Amanda. Betrayal. Itch. Bell Jar. Restaurant. Baby. Mother. Father. Betrayal. Amandabell. Restaurmatt. Father Jar. Betrayal. Virginity. Baby. Sex. Amanda. Sex. Mother. Itch. Sex. My whole everything is like one big live-action anagram. Or perhaps a sestina, a villanelle, a sonnet with its own peculiar pentameter, rhyming couplets, and grace notes. But what does it mean? Anything to anyone but me?

7/17

Dear Matt:

I am writing, using a "modern business letter format," to inform you that I am alive and well and, despite our last disagreement, thinking of you.

My mother has gone to visit her sister in California until further notice. I'm staying with my dad at my grandma's. See envelope for address.

I have, much to my chagrin, contracted what my physician has called late onset chicken pox.

You are welcome to visit. At any time. As I am without e-mail or private phone service, I'm hoping you can also, ahem, write.

I am, however, on the mend and, when well, look forward to seeing you at your earliest convenience.

Apologies again for my mysterious absence. So completely not my fault.

Sincerely yours,

Keek xoxo

DATE: July 18
MOOD: Incarcerated Rock Star
BODY TEMP: 101

This morning Gram gave me typing lesson number two: tabbing. It is not as hard as it looks, but it is also a lot harder than you might think. It is sofa king more efficient and accurate than pressing the space bar a million times.

My roots are showing.
    I have lost about ten pounds.
        Skinny and pockmarked like some kind of
        incarcerated rock star.

My fingers prance like rabbits on speed over the letters. It's entirely different from my mom's Mac with all the crud between the flat little keys. It's solid with its own mechanical business to do. It uses a ribbon cartridge! There's a little silver ball with all the letters and characters on it, like a Barbie-size disco ball spinning all my thoughts out and out and out as I can't stop typing because my fingers are caffeinated bunnies.

DO YOU UNDERSTAND MY RAPTURE??? THE
TYLENOL MUST BE KICKING IN.

Okay. Ouch. Shifting for that long is kinda hard, actually, but

```
will        it

            stop        me?


            NO!
```

I think I am actually developing a little muscle on the
side of my right wrist from all this TyPiNg. How's that for
fancy?

I asked Dad to mail my business letter to Matt this
morning, and I hope he didn't just leave it on the dashboard
to bleach in the white-hot sun with his take-out menus and
receipts. The idea that Matt might actually get my letter,
that I can communicate with him without any cyberspace
anything, is cheering me the hell up. Today I'm not even
that mad at him. No, today I am pooling my rage and anger
so I can spend it all on Amanda.

Amanda, it's true, is sort of hot, if you are into girls like
her. And if you are a stupid hormone-driven idiot like my
dad. My mom isn't chopped liver, though. She has longish
brown hair, not unlike a mermaid's, and her ears are pierced
more than once, which is a little lame but hot if you are

her age. Which is something I honestly do not know—more than forty and younger than fifty is my best guess. She is very amazing, and although she has abandoned her only daughter at this suburban version of the Bates Motel, she is, actually, or at least often is, my favorite person

Amanda. Ugh. If you were looking for the polar opposite of my mom, it would be her. (See chart.)

MOM	AMANDA
Brunette with auburn highlights	Blonde (greasy from pizza)
BA from University of Wisconsin	Triton Community College student
Triple-pierced ears	Tacky navel ring
Great family (Auntie, me, etc.)	Brother in jail for check fraud
Awesome boot collection	Ballet flats (cool, but still opposite)
Green eyes	Brown eyes
Been around the world	Been to Canada, once. Camping
Great cook (inspired, really)	Doesn't like fish because it's too fishy
Married to Dad	NOT married to Dad

I could go on and on and freaking on. But they are also opposite in ways that are more complicated. My mom works all the time. And when I say all the time, I mean every day and late at night and early in the morning. She doesn't even sit down to eat lunch because she is always on the go, and it makes her perpetually exhausted and angry.

There was a time, before my parents got the restaurant, when we actually went out to dinner. But the whole business is tainted now. Any place we go, Mom's always tallying how much profit they are clearing. Even at weddings and catered graduation parties, I can see the wheels in her brain clicking away, calculating their markup and wondering who did their draperies. Should she get a guy in to stencil some maps of Italy on the wall? Should she add a weekly pasta special or would that be too much for Jorge and Sebastian to handle in the kitchen?

She used to be more fun too before the D&D. We talked a lot more. She sang around the house and actually baked cookies once in a while. How Martha, I know. But the cookies were good, and it was fun and she was totally cool to be around.

Amanda, on the other hand, goes to community college part-time and works at the Dine & Dash. She goes to concerts downtown and sees lots of movies. She shops and buys (or occasionally shoplifts) expensive nail polish with stupid names. How noble. She screws married men for fun. That's about it. I don't think she even reads books.

!

Mom's the one who *hired* Amanda in the first place, which is possibly the most depressing thing ever. Mom said Amanda had "good energy" and would be "great with customers." Did my dad think, *Nice tits,* or, *How will she look wearing obscene lingerie, dancing in the walk-in freezer for an audience of cheese, bags of ice, and me?* That's where Mom said she found them, ridiculous underwear and all. Oh, the humanity.

What hurts so bad, and I mean <u>Bell Jar</u> bad, is that I really liked Amanda. Why I would befriend such an insane, undermining, manipulative whore from the underworld is beyond me. Before I found out about her and Dad, we were so close that she was the one who helped me bleach and dye my hair for the first time. Said she had done it before. Said, "It will look so much better than your hair now." Said, "What are you, chicken?"

Anything hair-related was something I would normally have done with Nic. She was my go-to style guru and we were always deeply involved in each other's evolving look. It's what we did together. But there was nothing normal about me at that point. Things at home with my parents fighting all the time and with Matt and our white-hot love were spiraling out of control.

At Amanda's apartment I sat in a folding chair with a towel over my shoulders as she wrapped hanks of my hair in tinfoil. She smoked half a pack of cigarettes while we ate low-fat pita chips with jarred salsa, waiting for the fuchsia to penetrate. I was transforming into a new person in her kitchen, trying to have power at least over the way I looked. And she let me sit there, like a dumb bunny, rinsing my hair in her sink and blow-drying it into shape as if she were my loving and loyal friend, instead of the person responsible for murdering my parents' marriage with an ax.

Amanda is also the one I spent at least eight hours a week working with at the D&D. Eight hours is a lot. It's more time than I spent with Matt during the week. More time than I spent with both my parents. I spent more time talking with Amanda, one-on-one about my life, than I did watching TV, for Christ's sake.

It's my own fault. I'm the one who decided she was so cool in the first place. I was fooled by her makeup, her well-placed eye rolling, her willingness to listen to me while I blathered on and on about Matt and school and books and all the rest. What choice did she have? I was her bosses' daughter. I had a choice, and I shouldn't have chosen her. I ignored the little things she did and said that made me uncomfortable, like making fun of my mom's jeans or taking quarters out of the register so she'd have enough to buy a pack of cigarettes at the 7-Eleven. It all seemed worth it to be in our girl gang of two, to hear her say "You're right," or "Got a light, Keekinator?" Making me feel like my life was as complex and subversive as I imagined it.

I used to have a real best friend. Nicola. She *is* nice. She does well in school. She is also a teenager, and we text and study together. She used to come over and we'd try new things like ratting our hair to make retro hairdos or concocting natural facial masks from organic ingredients found in our own kitchens. Nic is great. She is well-groomed and hell-bent on Northwestern or Princeton. She is lovely, decent, and for all intents and purposes exactly like me.

Amanda is not like me. She isn't in high school. No, she'd been through all that crap and come through it smelling like a rose. She was smart about things I knew nothing about, like craft beers and sex, and twenty-one-and-over shows. She had her own car and apartment. She had a job.

When we were together, I felt like I was finally sharing time with a like-minded individual. The thing is, my brain is not high school material. Why waste my time talking about SAT scores and homecoming and the latest homeroom scandal that no one over eighteen gives a rat's ass about?

Being with Amanda was—it was just amazing. She let me try smoking in the back when my parents weren't around. I didn't like it, but I loved just holding a cigarette between my fingers and staring into space like I was French and my heart was broken. It wasn't then, but it is now, and

Amanda, screw you. She's, I dunno, twenty-three, twenty-four. I mean, barely ten years older than me. When she was fifteen, I was five. So, okay, there's a large gap, but still. Too close for freaking comfort. Sick. Dad, you are a little sick. And I hate you. A little. And a bit more every day.

Some people, they just get it. They do what they say they will. They show up when it's important. They have integrity and genuine kindness and you can trust them with everything. Nic is one of these people. One thing is for sure, Nic would never have slept with my dad. The thought would never even have occurred to her in a million decades. Which is to say, a zillion billion years. An eon? An epoch? My eyes hurt and I am going to stop now so I can scratch the five places I am allowing myself to grate like cheese with my bitten-down nails.

MUTANT FROGBOY

Your hot tongue feels like
Laughter in my mouth
Alive.

Your smooth amphibian skin
Slides over me, silvery heat
More.

You are muscle and sinew
Supple and balanced seeking contact
Again.

DATE: July 19
MOOD: Dorian Grayian
BODY TEMP: 102

My name is Karina, so why doesn't anyone call me that? Keek. It's starting to sound like slang for urinating or puking. "Yo! Gotta take a keek." When I was little, I couldn't say "Karina," so when people asked me what my name was, I'd say "Keek" and then smile like a big dope while they all oohed and aahhed. Fast-forward thirteen years, and this is why I am fifteen and known to one and all as Keek. Don't make me keek.

I totally keeked last night. For real. Gram made me chicken soup and an egg salad sandwich and gave me a big glass of orange guava juice, which sounds total yum but at about ten thirty it was just the opposite. I didn't quite make it to the bathroom, because for a minute I didn't know where or who the hell I was. I thought I was home and that Mom and Dad were down the hall, but, duh, Dad was in the basement and Gram was watching the night rebroadcast of *Judge Judy*. As if being fifteen with the chicken pox isn't humiliating enough, I go puking down carpeted hallways.

I so take the body for granted. You need it to move around and stuff. To bring thought to action. I'm all about my brain. I often think I would be more than happy to be a brain in a jar hooked up with electrodes like in sci-fi movies from the 1960s. Then I could keep myself amused for decades with my own mental blathering, or at least figure out how to take over the world with my understanding of The Bell Jar and rudimentary applications of sine and cosine.

But here I am, weak and skinny, and I'm seeing health as something exotic. Wrestlers have intense strength and bulldog tenacity. Cheerleaders—whom I, perhaps unfairly, mock—can command their bodies to do splits, backbends, and hula-colorful-hoops around their hips, and barely break a sweat. The picture of health. I am like Dorian Gray: From afar I look like your average pink-cheeked teen, but on closer inspection, the blush is from fever and I'm covered in weeping sores like a leper waiting for Jesus. Christ! And so freaking itchy.

I need my poor itchy body. Even though it betrays me all the time. Cancer cells could be lurking in my breasts right this second and only cause trouble when I'm in my fifties. My body could also derail my whole vague virginity plan with its own agenda, like it did that midsummer's night in Matt's room last June.

Oh, God. That midsummer night in Matt's room.

Let me just say that last summer we had only been going out for a little while, but long enough to know that we were crazy for each other in a new and extreme way that surprised us both. Matt invited me to his parents' annual *A Midsummer Night's Dream* party. His parents are the biggest geeks around. His dad is some kind of executive networker and attends a lot of galas and fund-raisers downtown. His mom's an optometrist with a thing for Shakespeare in the Park. His house is enormous, and the yard is even bigger. His parents must be surprised that their only son is such a jock. That he needs help with his English essays. That he doesn't need eyeglasses. Needless to say, Matt's parents really like me. A lot.

I showed up to their big annual garden gala in a white sundress and a flower behind my ear. There were giant paper lanterns dripping light all over the backyard, glowing pale yellow and pink and lavender like miniature moons. Fireflies twinkled at our fingertips. Most of the guests wore costumes, the women in fairy wings like oversize kindergartners, and garlands of flowers around their necks. The men went for a troubadour/Renaissance faire/Hobbit look with sandals and peasant shirts. In two words: Awe. Some.

And then Matt took me by the elbow and pointed toward the garage, where this skinny guy with a giant papier-mâché donkey head started skipping among the guests, tossing flower petals from a basket slung over his arm and braying—like HEE-HAWing. "My mom gave him fifty bucks to do that," Matt said.

The donkey came over, took its head off, and it was—who the hell else?—Earl the Squirrel, sweaty, out of breath, and already half-drunk, laughing, er, his head off.

"Hey, Keek," he said like he was actually glad to see me, and then to Matt, "Dude. You haven't lived until you have been a Bottom," and then he cracked up again, glitter sticking to his forehead.

"Don't be an ass," I said, and we were all giggling like idiots, and I hadn't had anything to drink yet.

Earl went to find food, and Matt brought me and a bottle of wine to his room so we could drink and talk and watch the lovesick fairies in the garden eat stuffed mushrooms and talk about the stock market under white Christmas tree lights.

"Cool party," I said. We were sitting on his bed swigging from the bottle like pirates. Up until then we'd only been able to make out on park benches like French people. Or in his car, or in the back of the D&D. We hadn't even been at each other's houses or anything official like that. But it was clear we were into each other and an actual couple, and there we were—on his bed. His room was semi-tidy and had a soccer ball in one corner and an empty fish tank in another. The wine was delicious. Or maybe after the first twelve sips I just got used to it. I'm so like Esther that way, hoping that one day I'll wake up and think that alcohol actually tastes good and not like poison. It—and I mean the whole situation—was on fire with amazingness.

"Cool party if you're into that stuff. Shakespeare, I mean. You are, right?" He was so beautiful. He had a little glitter on him, too and his lips were dark from the wine. I was into anything he wanted me to be into. And what kind of honors English student would I be if I didn't adore Shakespeare?

"Yeah." My voice was weird, low and husky. When I saw him take a book out of his back pocket, dear reader, I almost passed the hell out. Because then?

He.

Started.

To.

Read.

To.

Me.

A FREAKING SONNET.

Do I remember which one? Does it matter? There were thees and thous, enigmatic questions, and he had one knee on the bed, and then both, and then an elbow, and then we were rolling around on top of his sheets. My sundress, made of white cotton, became just another sheet, and off it came, so I was just lounging on his bed in my underwear, which was rather like a bikini.

How did I get practically naked? Your guess is as good

as mine. It's like he Googled "How to seduce an honors English virgin" and was testing his new romancing skills on me. I was lying there all ready to let Matt gather ye rosebuds. No, really. My body was on autopilot. My brain was in the back room with the dishwashers taking a smoke break, and the inner rubber band that usually kept my knees together had just snapped in two. Everything—every breath, kiss, eyelash flutter on my neck—felt so good that you could have taken a knife and sliced me from stem to stern and I would have loved it.

But then there was a knock on the door, and my dress was back on fairy-magic fast, desperately holding on to my shoulders with two pathetic spaghetti straps, and there was Earl the Squirrel, leaning in the doorway, holding a paper plate of artichoke dip and toast points, saying, "Wherefore art thou, Romeo, yo?"

Matt was all nonchalant, running a hand over his bangs and stretching in an obnoxious and over-the-top way to draw attention away from his RAGING ERECTION.

Am I glad that Earl showed up? I guess. I mean, yeah. But not really. The thing about my virginity is that I want it to be taken from me—like pick-pocketed from my purse on the bus. No. I don't want to be raped or anything sick like that, but I also don't want to have to mull it over and make a big conscious decision about my course of action. But if my virginity is snatched—tugged gently from my neck like a diamond necklace by a handsome highwayman in the middle of the night—that would be great. I want to be in control and out of control at the same time. Which I know is irrational, a little gutless, and not really like me, but when it comes to the maidenhead, I am a big chickenshit.

Besides, Earl's *WTF?* face in the doorway, chewing with his mouth open, was never in one of the millions of virginity-losing scenarios I had imagined.

So I got up. Scrunched my hair up in my fingers for that bed-head look, slipped on my flip-flops, and went back out to the party, my insides all jittery and my pulse thumping through my ears like soldiers on the march. I made small talk with adults. I quoted Shakespeare. Once in a while I held Matt's hand and blushed because I wanted to kiss him with my entire body under the stars on that beautiful night.

Now Matt and I are very familiar with each other's houses. He knows where we keep the snacks and that the Cokes are in the back of the fridge. Coffee galumphs down the carpeted stairs when Matt comes over, falling all over herself, for a belly rub. But it is that first star-flecked night that I still think of before I fall asleep, the lazy nonchalance of it. No one ever told me that finding out about bodies and what I like and what I want from boys—men, whatever—was supposed to be fun or that it was a moderately joyful process. It always seemed fraught with secrecy and shame. Pregnancy terrifies me. Betrayal terrifies me. And how insane howl-at-the-moon lusty I get whenever Matt breathes on my neck is a little scary too. That night was the only time things felt different. And easier. Why do I make everything so complicated?

Still, when I see Matt tug off his ear guards after a wrestling match and his hair goes all spiky and he looks for me in the stands and winks, I remember the sheets and the fireflies and savor it like a butterscotch candy in my mouth, clicking it around my teeth. When I am old, I will probably remember that twinkling night more than other more naked and debauched nights that might never happen.

But that night was a year ago already. And although I get a little brazen once in a while and I have been expanding my comfort zone with Matt millimeter by millimeter every day, I still panic and freak-the-hell-out just when things get *really* interesting. When my bones go rubbery and my mind slows down with desire, I'm all "Later, alligator," gone in a flash.

I'm making my (non)sex life up as I go along. That night in his room at the beginning of our relationship would have been the best possible time for Matt to reveal what he waited more than a year to tell me. If only he had told me *then* instead of *last week*. If I were writing the screenplay of my life, that is the place where I would have sofa king put it.

AMANDA THE TWO-FACED TRAMP

Unasked, you harvest
My weaknesses and wounds,
My anxieties and girlish blunders,
My teenage dread and virginal dreams,
Gingerly placing each one,
Hot, private, painful,
Into a Tupperware box.
A heartbreak snack
For later,
To launch at me in sopping, bloody chunks
Before you slink away
And fuck my father in the freezer.

DATE: July 20
MOOD: Twice Shy
BODY TEMP: 101

I am too embarrassed to talk to anyone about my family.
Except Matt, and for all I know, he has the hots for Amanda
too. I wouldn't put it past him. See where my brain is? Why
am I able to type my guts out without fatigue but hardly
have the energy to drag myself to the bathroom or sit up
to drink the tea that Gram brings me each afternoon? And
when I finally fall asleep, I have nightmares about babies in
jars. Or Amanda, ripping open my neck and filling a beer
stein with my blood at a vampire bar on the North Side of
Chicago. She invades my brain all the time, and I'm sick
of it. I can't help but try to figure out when I should have
started to mistrust her, to become suspicious. Why was I so
addicted to her?

Amanda and I went shopping together, often. In malls.
Like teenagers in John Hughes movies. (Nicola calls malls
"mals," as in French for "bad.") My best-est in the west-est
new pal Amanda and I bought stupid jewelry and T-shirts

with ironic sayings. Afterward she—real—and I—pretend—
smoked in her car, listening to her iPod via the car lighter
adapter.

Listening to Amanda's music was like being inside her
brain. She always had it on shuffle, so it was like a trip
through her entire life there in her crappy used hatchback,
or whatever it was, with pennies all over the floor. There
was corny musical music from *Guys and Dolls* (which she
was in, in high school; a Hot Box girl, sofa king textbook),
heavy-bass techno stuff, reggae, and some really old punk
from her ex-boyfriend, who used to be in a mediocre band
that supposedly played at the Double Door all the time.

Even though most of it was benign, every song made me
think of sex. And not just sex in movies or ridiculous Internet
porn, but bodies in general. There in her car I remember
thinking that people—and by "people" I mean me, Amanda,
my parents, rock stars, baristas, CNN reporters, etc.—are
free, for the most part, to do whatever they want. As long
as no one gets hurt. How cool is that? AS LONG AS NO
ONE GETS HURT.

Every time one song faded into the next, I fake inhaled
and exhaled plumes of renegade smoke, thinking of
Amanda dancing backstage in leather pants or emerging
spectacularly from a pool in Las Vegas wearing a bikini,
water cascading over her navel ring. This is probably how
my father thought about her too as he delivered pizzas all

over the western suburbs. Ugh. Absolutely disgusting.

Matt's parents have a walnut-paneled basement with an upholstered white leather L-shaped couch. The corner of the *L*—well, let's just say I like the corner of the *L* and Matt loves the corner of the *L*. We are currently at a stand-off about how much further we'll go in the corner of the *L*, because there is not really much further we can go without going through with it.

I'm an only child, okay? If I had a sister or something I would have talked about this with her instead of my parents' employee, who, unbeknownst to me, was about to embark on a covert plan of sleeping with my father and ruining my life and my mom's life and everything else in the process.

So imagine, talking with this very person about very intense, intimate things like the taste of a boy's penis (!) and orgasms (?) and what am I supposed to do, and basically revealing how, despite my smarts, wisdom, and cynical dis-regard for mundane behavior, I am so inexperienced with this real-world stuff that it's entirely embarrassing.

What the hell would Nic have contributed to this conver-sation? Probably a lot. Probably would have asked me what I thought was important. Asked me why I was so scared. Told me I should probably take a break if it was freaking me out so much, because I wasn't quite ready. Basically she would have made me feel like an absolute *CHILD*, which is why I didn't talk about it with her in the first place. So instead I told that wise, empathetic, and loving dirtbag Amanda all this stuff with total trust, respect, and high regard, desperate to hear what she had to say about my sexual misadventures on Matt's L-shaped couch.

Amanda and I had this disturbingly intense friendship. It felt like there were no real barriers between us. We were both young women, we liked the same kind of music, she really knew my parents—and not in passing, like other friends. She worked with us—me, Jorge, and Sebastian—and knew things like how far to fill the soap dispenser in the men's room and how the one steamer wand on the cappuccino machine had to get really hot before it made enough steam for a cup, how my mom liked total silence in the restaurant for five minutes before it opened, to "gather her energy."

We had our own slang for stuff. Amanda's the one who started saying "sofa king" all the time, and now I can't stop saying it or typing it. We were trying to figure out a way to swear without freaking out customers, and that was her genius idea. And I thought it was the most amazing play on words ever.

She even told me that she had read The Bell Jar when she was in high school and thought it was—are you ready?—"so rad." *RAD?* As in neato? Gnarly? Peachy-freaking-keen?

How could I not see then that she did not take me as seriously as I took her? In The Bell Jar, Esther has this so-called friend Doreen, who is a tramp (in a bad way) and whose breasts pop out of her strapless dress while she dances (drunk) with a singing cowboy, and she doesn't even notice. Doreen is also selfish and gossipy and mean and probably not nice to her mother. She is also unlike all of Esther's nice friends. The kindhearted, talented, Nicola-esque ones who are eager to please and nice to their parents.

How Esther felt with Doreen is how I felt being with Amanda: sarcastic and cool and more alive than other people. Amanda wanted to get really close to me right away, like best friends at first sight, just like Doreen was with Esther. And Doreen and Amanda are both truly hilarious. That's how Esther got reeled in. Although it is comforting to think that Esther went through this kind of thing too, it still makes me wonder.

Why, oh why, did I like Amanda so much?

Is this some kind of universal growing up/girl-on-girl crime rite of passage that all women go through? Seriously?

I didn't get the e-mail alert.

Dad's home.

Gotta keek.

DATE: July 21
MOOD: Off-Kilter
BODY TEMP: 101

Gram tripped over the typewriter cord last night when she came to check on me, and I thought for a second as she fell toward me that she was (a) trying to strangle me or (b) having a heart attack. She's not, like, old-old or anything, but I just wasn't expecting such a dramatic entrance. Gram is really quiet. She stares into space while she smokes, but she doesn't look French or heartbroken at all. She looks frozen, like someone pressed pause on the DVD player, except that the smoke is still moving. It's really creepy. Her husband (my grandpa) was sort of a grade-A nonorganic jerk and left her when she was young with a little kid (my dad) for a much younger woman. Do you see how my whole life is like an elaborately painted Russian nesting doll?

My pox are expanding, fattening with itch, then spreading and flattening, and then disappearing. Slowly. But then new ones pop up, and I feel like I will be in this calico-curtained bedroom beneath this typewriter for the rest of my life. Illness makes you forget things. Like what day it is. I am, obviously, in my own little typing world while my body fights the pox. I'm not even watching TV, really. Well, last night I wrapped a blanket around my shoulders and shuffled to the front room like the Creature from the Black Lagoon to watch the late rebroadcast of *Judge Judy* with Gram.

I think if my grandma could do it all over again, she would like to have ended up more like Judge Judy and a little less like herself. JJ is as tough as she can be but still have people like her. She is very fair. Her Honor doesn't like liars, cheats, or weak girls who let stupid men take advantage of them. She is a champion for children. And her dark brown eyes will burn you to a crisp if you mistakenly treat her like your run-of-the-mill sweet old lady. Which she is so not.

My grandma isn't like that at all. She doesn't look people square in the eye when they talk to her, even me sometimes. She worries a lot. About the battery in the smoke detector dying. What to make for dinner (which is actually rather important when caring for a pox-afflicted, and often hallucinating, teenager). Other worries—for example, her son living in her basement for the rest of his life; her only granddaughter, who is kind of fragile right now; her daughter-in-law, aka my mother, and their pending relationship—these don't seem to faze her. Gram even told me once before Dad's hideous infidelity, "I couldn't have asked for a better daughter." (Note: She did not say daughter-*in-law*.)

So she is not only gaining a midlife adulterous, nonpaying tenant, she is also losing a daughter.

How am I supposed to digest that? What is family anyway but people who are always supposed to be there for you? Family should be rock solid, the earth beneath your feet, wind beneath your wings, and all that. What do I do, now that it's not? I'm dog-paddling here with the pox, just treading water until this sea of betrayal washes me back to shore so I can function like the earthbound mammal I am. I mean, Christmas is screwed. I can't imagine opening presents without my dad there, for Christ's sake. The very idea of never sitting at the same table again with both my mother and my grandmother just makes me want to scurry into the nearest crawl space with a bottle of pills. It's even harder to imagine my mom and dad not eating together, because of the restaurant. They are always around food or preparing food or delivering food. Thinking about my disintegrating family made me sob and sob and cry my freaking eyes out under the hundred-pound coverlet after watching JJ.

I wish this all wasn't happening, but it is. My dad drags his feet into Gram's house looking at the floor, as if that's where he's going to discover the secret to restoring everything to the way it used to be.

When I lie on the couch, he pats me on the head. Says, "Feeling any better, Keek?" not waiting for an answer. He stabs a fork into a bowl of cold pasta Gram left out for him before she went to bed. He drinks a tall glass of milk alone at the kitchen table like a boy from the 1950s having an after-school snack, and I know for certain that my mother can't take him back. He has hurt us all too much. He seems smaller to me, his shoulders slumped, his face long. I want to pat him on the shoulder or crawl into his lap like a kid and ask him to read me a story with a happy ending. But he hasn't even sat me down for the big heart-to-heart that all guidance counselors recommend to shepherd your only child through a divorce, an event that will transform her entire life and affect all her future relationships. Like losing my virginity, my parents' splitting up is an event for which there will forever be a defined before and after. And that's not even factoring in the devastation of Amanda's faux friendship and betrayal, my own trust and love and sex issues with Matt, which Dad doesn't even *know* about. Or the sad fact that I have accidentally on purpose estranged myself from my true friends. And my mom isn't even here for me to cry to, talk with, etc.

You know how when you have the flu or are extremely tired it feels like there is melted lava in your bones and it hurts to move? Well, that is how I felt last night while I watched JJ for twenty minutes, daydreaming of justice. I imagined my mom and I were the plaintiffs. Dad and Amanda, the defendants. Gram, Nic, Matt, Jorge, Sebastian, and Mrs. Dougherty, my fifth-grade English teacher, were in the audience, rooting for us. Amanda wore her most ridiculous and low-waisted polyester suit from H&M. Dad wore an apron covered in Italian beef juice over his suit—the suit he wore to my eighth-grade graduation ceremony. Mom and I looked good, really good, and my hair didn't have brown roots and I didn't feel sad or pitiful or furious or depressed, because Her Honor Judge Judy Sheindlin looked exactly like Sylvia Plath on the inside cover of The Bell Jar, Harper Perennial 2006 edition, with the pearls and the smile and the bun in her hair. JJ read Dad the riot act and she was merciless.

"How dare you?" she asked. "What kind of stinkin' thinkin' goes on in the back room of your restaurant? Don't spit on my cupcake and tell me it's frosting. Excuse me. I'm talking to you, Bozo." Basically all the things I wanted to say to my dad but haven't. Everything was out in the open. Everyone knew what had gone on at the Dine & Dash. Everyone saw how Mom and I were women wronged and once this trial was over, once judgment was passed, fees were levied, sentences were meted out, we could all go home and start over again, like in movies when families enter the witness protection program.

"And you, the wrestler," Judge Judy said suddenly, talking to Matt, "don't piss on my leg and tell me it's raining. You misrepresented yourself. You owe this girl an apology." And just as I was about to address the court and make my closing arguments, both sides of my abdomen seized up with cramps, and each and every single pock, and there are about a hundred, itched as if there were a thousand fleas all over my body.

And I realized that I felt especially bad not just because I, um, *have the chicken pox,* and my parents are *splitting up* and my *so-called boyfriend* seems to have *fallen off the face of the earth,* and someone I thought was a *friend stabbed* me in the back about a thousand times like a serial killer, and my mother is in California visiting a *dying* infant with a *lightbulb-shaped brain*—aka my brand-new *cousin*—but hooray, hooray, caloo, callay, I also have my freaking *period.*

DATE: July 22
MOOD: Red as Sylvia's Bedside Tulips
BODY TEMP: 101.5

Oh, the humanity.

Today did not begin well. First of all, I am weak. It's hard to support myself on what feel like linguini legs, let alone brush my hair or put on some lip gloss. Or talk on the phone. But Mom called, and I practically fell head over heels like a mouse in a cartoon to get to the telephone.

Hearing her on the phone was surreal. She was the bass player and backup singer in a band in college and has a really nice voice. Melodious, really, but I'm her daughter and am missing her so much that if I weren't so sick, I'd be embarrassed. I tried to be cool and not lay my itchy forehead on the desk and weep like a baby. She had a lot to tell me, and here is a list:

1. The weather in California is *hot*, and because of the smog, the sun doesn't really come out until noon in LA, which is especially depressing to

    my mother at this particular moment in her life.

2. The baby has gained seven ounces since Mom got there, and the doctors are what they call "cautiously optimistic."

3. The baby is a *girl*. (But of course she is. All of the boys in my family married in.)

4. Auntie has named her: Aurora. I know. Like freaking Sleeping Beauty, but whatev. It's sort of sophisticated, and maybe the *Sleeping Beauty* reference was totally on purpose, which just dawned on me this very second.

5. Aurora has jaundice. She is yellow and under lights. She has respiratory distress syndrome because her lungs weren't totally developed when she was born, but they should be, soon. And she has prongs smaller than TicTacs in her nostrils to keep the tubes supplying oxygen in place.

6. I've been asked to pray for Aurora, although everyone knows I'm not a pray-er. I will anyway.

7. Mom said two things while whispering as if she didn't want anyone to hear, and they were:
   - Aurora looks like a boiled Cornish hen.
   - How's your dad doing?

How's that for fancy tabbing and bulleting on this practically prehistoric typewriter? How's Dad doing? Why should she care about how he's doing? And thanks, Mom, for replacing the Hobbit-in-formaldehyde image with a chicken-on-life-support visual. I refuse to freak out about the baby. If the baby dies, we might as well just pack it in and pull a Sylvia Plath, sticking our heads into our ovens and waiting for the eternal blackness. The worst thing is that there's nothing I can do to help, like give blood or make coffee or paint my aunt's toenails with yellow (Lemonade Stand by Your Man) and black (Caviar) nail polish so it looks like leopard spots, which I did that time we all went to visit her in California.

I mean, I was a little premature when I was born. Not by months or anything, but a few weeks. I was skinny, probably slightly chicken-esque. I made it, obviously, and Aurora will too. She's one of us. She has to live through this. If I have to, Aurora has to. The scary thing is, my mom cried a little bit before we hung up, a little sniffling and hard swallowing. A lot has been going on for a long time with our family, but I haven't heard her cry like that since the night Dad moved out. God. These parents of mine are worse than teenagers. Hello? Is this mike on? I am the teenager here. Me. With the *chicken pox*. And the *divorcing* parents, and the boyfriend from *Ragin Hormone High*. And *they* are crying. WTF?

I have a totally high tolerance for gore and otherwise vile things. They just don't skeeve me out like your average girl. I'm not *into* gross things, like an eight-year-old boy who would be fascinated by pus and boogers and grasshopper-eating villagers in Mexico, okay? I'm more like an ER doctor or a combat medic. There is some philosopher we read about in English who said, "Nothing human is foreign to me," or something like that (not like I can even Google it in this *Little House on the Prairie*), and I'm that way about body stuff. No problem with the dissection in biology; no problem cleaning up after Coffee when she had that intestinal reaction to her heartworm pills.

Once when my dad was really sick with the flu, he vomited every twenty minutes. My mom—you know, his then-wife—was physically unable to clean up after him without dry-heaving herself, so it fell to me. And it was no big deal. At the restaurant, when Jorge is busy busing tables, I'm often the one who hoses out the Dumpster, which actually gets hot from the anaerobic respiration of rotting food in the corners. I'm the one who is expected to clean up all the messes, and maybe I'm a little burnt out from it. Maybe I want a transfer. Maybe I'd like to give two weeks' notice. Maybe I need a freaking vacation and getting chicken pox was the only way to do it, people.

This is the long way of saying that it was not the blood that freaked me out. It was forgetting that I was expecting it. I was so sick, I thought I was eight instead of almost sixteen. Good God. I got up to go to the bathroom, and it was as if an otter had been slaughtered in the center of my bed. I had to grab on to the dresser to keep from keeling over, but knocked the clock radio onto the floor in the process. Which is what brought Gram running.

Behold! The blood! And not just the big stain, but all the random polka dots of pox oozings. How disgusting. And do you know what my Grandma said?

She said: "Oh, my poor baby." Which is the nicest thing anyone has ever said to me my whole life. At least that is how it felt. And she gave me a real hug as I swooned. She walked me to the bathroom, sat me on the toilet. She started the water for a bath—hot. She ripped open an Aveeno soothing bath treatment and poured it under the tap. (*Soulage l'irritation et la demangeaison*: Relieves itchy, irritated skin. *Sans parfum*.) She told me to raise my arms above my head, and she tugged my nightgown, one of Matt's giant T-shirts, over my head and then pulled my blood-soaked underwear down to my ankles and helped me step out of them.

These were things that my father could never in a million years have done to help me. It was the most personal and private thing I have ever done with anybody, even my mom. Even Matt. I was so weak and helpless, it didn't even occur to me to be embarrassed or modest. Of *course* Gram was once fifteen. Of *course* she has seen worse. Of *course* she loves me more than she says out loud.

I stepped over the edge of the porcelain tub and held

on to her hands as I lowered myself into the milky water like a lasagna noodle. The itching stopped. Ribbons of pink swirled up, and I let the steam settle on my face. Gram kissed the top of my head and told me to lean forward. She dunked a washcloth into this slightly disgusting, yet oddly cleansing, hot water and rubbed it over my back and rib cage and neck, which felt so good I thought I was going to pass out.

In <u>The Bell Jar</u> Esther is totally into baths, especially when she is miserable and lonely. When she is nervous or depressed, she hunches down below the water line and waits for the bath to cure her. My bath didn't really cure anything, but it was, in its way, totally transformative.

So when I stood to get out and blood poured down my wet legs, I didn't really care. I was totally without shame or anything. Gram used a towel to dry me off and found a fresh pair of my underwear and a menstrual apparatus that she said she'd been holding on to "for a moment just like this." Even though I felt like crap, we both stood there giggling our heads off. Clean itch-free body, clean nightgown, clean sheets, two Tylenol, and I slept for fourteen hours.

In.

A.

Row.

Ahhhhhhh.

DATE: July 23
MOOD: Retrospective
BODY TEMP: 101.5

Last semester, right before my life went all <u>Bell Jar</u>ian and we were a starry-eyed and crazy-in-love new couple, Matt made fifteen hundred dollars by drinking revolting things at lunch. Wrestlers have to make weight all the time, and like everything else body related, Matt was extremely talented at knowing how to keep things in his stomach and how to get them out.

It started right before winter break. The guys were all sitting around eating their stupid protein bars and salads with chicken and ice-cream cups and whatever else wrestlers eat the week before nationals. Matt had a tall glass of milk, not glass-glass but plastic, the pebbled-shower-door-looking kind. They were impersonating Coach Pernaki and his insistence on healthy weight maintenance. "Try a tofu, fruit, and yogurt smoothie before a workout, son. Add a raw egg for extra protein."

Then someone on the team said, "A little ketchup, for

stamina," and squirted ketchup (spelled "catsup" on the packets at school, which totally infuriates me) into Matt's milk.

"Yeah, and Italian dressing!" Into the milk it went. And on and on. Peanut butter, Orange Crush, gravy from the Salisbury steak.

"Drink it, Matt," Earl the Squirrel said. (Who else would want to see that?) "Five bucks you can't."

"Make it ten."

"Twenty he can't do it," and on and on until three tables of jocks were gathered around Matt's lunch table clutching money in their hands like strung-out poker addicts.

Matt waited. He eyed the glass. He took a spoon. And stirred. He stood and, holding the glass aloft so light from the windows played upon the vile slop within, he held it to his mouth and drank it down in six giant gulps. He kissed two of his fingers and pointed to God. We had different lunch periods, but I have heard the story so many times I could make a YouTube video of it using sock puppets and a Barbie doll.

Because I wasn't there and didn't actually witness it, Matt's lunchtime exploits came to me through the awestruck whispers of other students. He was a celebrity. A legend. A mythical creature with ingestion skills of epic proportions. Already popular, Matt became the one person everyone was interested in. Freshmen, sophomores, juniors, even seniors were fascinated with what was in his glass, and The Swallowing became an event. And it was awesome. And it made me think Matt was fearless and smart and totally antiestablishment, and I loved it.

Every Friday, Matt drank whatever was put before him. People started to bring in things from home: soy sauce, Tabasco, hummus. The base was always milk, and bets started at five bucks. He was saving up for a laptop, so it wasn't all pointless, but he could have paid for his first year at U of I if the principal hadn't heard about the wagering and shut down the whole operation. It was amazing, being the girlfriend of the boy who would drink anything. It made him, and me by association, famous. And being famous was something I liked. Being known. Significant. Walking to my locker while girls looked away, suddenly bashful in the presence of a fascinating enigma: me.

I had never had a boyfriend before Matt, really. I'd had friends. That were boys. Oh, I'd gone on dates to dances, Sno-Ball, Valentine's, Sock-Hop, et al, just like Sylvia and Esther and Buddy and their ilk went to Yale proms, senior formals, debutante balls, etc.

There are a lot of schools in our suburb. There's our high school and the all girl's Catholic college prep school and the boys-only quasi-military academy and two junior highs, all within the same zip code. Nicola and I were friends with all types of kids in the neighborhood, and in eighth grade got asked to tons of school dances by all the guys we knew. "No strings, Keek. Promise," they'd say.

The thing about dances is that there are rules. You wear a dress. The boy wears a suit. The boy, bearing a corsage in a plastic container like a pet hamster in an exercise ball, picks you up at your house. Pictures are taken. A curfew is mentioned. Your parents know who, what, where, when, and why, especially in eighth grade, when parents are the ones who have to drive you there and pick you up.

You dance to a DJ, and sometimes it's in a big group and fun, like the Hokey Pokey but with more touching. And punk rock. The gym is always decorated with crepe paper and balloons, or the colonnade room is decorated with Christmas lights and tulle. You drink punch. If you are me, you desperately try to make small talk while slow dancing, pretending you are an extra on a rerun of *The Love Boat* because you no-freaking-way want this nice boy to think you have the hots for him just because you wanted to go to a dance. All you want is to have fun without having to get attached and emotional about some boy you learned how to write cursive with in the third grade. When you get home, you put the corsage in the refrigerator. Just in case you want to wear it the next day. And then Nic comes over in the morning and you rehash the whole night over organic pancakes and Earl Grey tea.

Sure, I kissed a few of them. Only one with tongue—

not because I wanted to, but I had to thrust back with my own to keep his the hell out. It was like an alien probe, for real. He was new at it—and bad at it. I know just how bad because Matt is superior. Matt knows what the hell he is doing, could teach a class at The Learning Annex on how to make a girl's knees buckle without even trying.

So not only was Matt my capital-B Boyfriend, but I was into being his and his being mine. Proud of it. Out of all the people in the world, or at least our high school, we found each other.

"Karina," he said right after our very first kiss, "I've never met a girl like you before." And when I'm with him, I feel unique and extraordinary, and I love surprising him by being myself.

At first I assumed he was exactly like the thousands of other Jocks I Have Known. But once I got to know him better, I realized that what I saw was the tip of the freaking iceberg. Brave, funny, a little cynical, into art. Matt is his own person, an individual. When he was in the hospital for kidney stones, I brought him a sea monkey kit to keep him occupied, and he thought it was as hilarious as I did.

I wanted the universe to know of our love, that we were thiscloseto doing it so watch and be in awe, because no one has ever been us or felt like us. We roamed the halls together like feral wolves. Standing in the hallway between the cafeteria and the gym, Matt would press my body against his by holding on to the thick strap on my book bag. Then his other hand would be heavy on my neck, fingers entwined in my hair. And we'd kiss like ravenous blind people, trying to see from our throats. Our bodies radiated heat as we walked from our lockers to the parking lot.

When we were together, we were all that mattered. When the bell rang, we'd go to our separate classes and I'd write my name and his inside hearts like a unicorn-loving idiot. I swear. I couldn't help it. Just thinking of his hands around my waist made me have to put my head on my desk to catch my breath. I felt all the time like Esther, while skiing downhill for the very first time, thinking that she was the happiest she had ever been. Just before she broke her leg.

This was right before the black hair, before the pink hair, before Amanda and the freezer, graffiti tights, keyboarding class, the pox. Before this disastrous summer. Nic and I were still talking every day, still laughing when I would call her name down the hall like the yodelers in that Ricola cough drop commercial, "Neeeee-co-laaaah."

I'll always remember those last days when my life was airy and exciting and I was the most famous girl in school who got to eat free food at the Dine & Dash with the coolest, most accomplished wrestler on the team, a boy whose every motion in life was part of a larger effort to get me into his beautiful bed. Before Dad moved out. Before Mom started meditating herself to sleep every night. Before now.

You know the saying "It's darkest before the dawn,"

right? Well, for me it was as bright as the freaking sun before the meteor hit.

I was ablaze with happiness.

And then things fell apart.

When I had the mumps back in February, they weren't as bad as the chicken pox. Ah. The mumps. The temporarily disfiguring childhood illness mocked in Three Stooges movies. I got them right around when Matt figured out exactly how far I would let his hand down my pants or into my bra before I jumped up in terror of my own desire and went home.

It was also the time when my beloved parents went into weekly counseling. They came home late and went to bed early on Wednesday nights while I ate flamin' hot Cheetos and drank Dr Pepper and read and reread and read one more time The Bell Jar because it was the only thing that seemed real.

What was so weird about couples therapy (or whatever people are calling it nowadays) was all the sex they were having. Like most normal people, I don't think about my parents', er, lovemaking. As a kid I never walked in on them, or if I did, I didn't realize it. I had never heard them before, but I did during those months of Wednesday night marriage analysis.

In the eye of the storm that was the breakup of their marriage, they did it all the time. And I could *hear them*. Moaning and thrusting, stifled yelps of laughter and pleasure, mattress squeaking, and all the other ridiculous comedy tropes you can imagine. Was it so wrong of me to think of this as a good sign? They were, after all, together. Making the love. A lot. But perhaps they were making the hate. Saying good-bye the way rabbits make bunnies.

This and all other kinds of heartbreaking and distracting crap was weakening my defenses, making me susceptible to whatever diseases I hadn't had the good fortune to previously contract. Whooping cough, diphtheria, scarlet-freaking-fever. Congratulations, mumps! You made it past the velvet rope of my immune system. School was school. I wasn't doing so hot in math and biology, but was sailing through honors English as usual.

The mumps are *hilarious*. For real. One minute I felt fine, a little giddy and hot to the touch, but not achy or nauseous or in any way bad. I looked good, cheeks flushed like Heidi, as if I'd been foraging for mushrooms in the Alps. But by ten thirty, I started to feel a little weird. Then dizzy. I was in a fantastic mood. Happy for a change, laughing and giggling as I asked the school nurse if I could call home. They didn't believe that I was sick, but let me use the phone anyway. Good grades do that to a person, make them invincible to school personnel.

As I sat on the couch in the health office waiting for Mom, my neck started to feel tight. It was getting hard to swallow. I lay my head back and tee-heed at the ridiculousness of the nurse phoning in an order for paper cups and memo pads, the Garfield on her JUST HANG IN THERE poster leering at me like a bulge-eyed kidney patient awaiting dialysis.

When Mom showed up an hour later (it's hard to just up and leave the D&D during the lunch rush), she took one look at me and started to laugh. She was practically rolling on the floor guffawing and holding her stomach as she led me to the car.

My mom. She's great, but she's also pretty into her own "trajectory." She has this elaborate theory about her place in the universe and ways to take care of her own "life's purpose." She's always downloading guided meditations for things like "Clearing Blockages" and "Transcending Your Ego" and "Accelerating Your Evolution." Right after my parents started counseling, I was always catching her mid-Zen, her iPod nano clipped to her shirt collar—earbuds in, eyes half-open, all zoned-out to some guru like she was stoned.

I listened to one of them once. A woman with a smooth

jazz DJ voice encouraged me to "open to receive," and to "let the light of your soul radiate light up to the light," all with this New Age music box tinkling in the background.

Now, if we lived in California or if my mom had ever once in her life worn Birkenstocks, this would have made more sense. But my mom meditating was like the Dalai Lama mugging old ladies as they got off the El. It didn't quite add up. She was all punk rock, once. She used to be edgier—meaning her edges were sharper, her sense of humor more cynical. Then she'd just seemed preoccupied and nervous. At least the meditating seemed to calm her down. She told me she was putting the "om in 'mom.'" Isn't she clever?

It felt good to see her laugh that mumps day. If it had been anyone else, I would have been annoyed as hell. But it was my mom. And for some reason—a lot of reasons, I guess—it's really hard for me to get mad and stay mad at her.

Anyway, I think if I'd felt awful, I would have been outraged at her totally un-motherly behavior, but Mom is as charismatic as Jesus, and I was laughing too, just because she was laughing. When we got to the car, she said, "Honey, have you looked at yourself?"

So I looked in the rearview mirror and—like Esther Greenwood seeing her reflection for the first time after her suicide attempt—I didn't recognize myself. I looked like a chipmunk storing a winter's worth of *nuts* in my *cheeks*. My head formed a perfect *triangle*. I looked *inhuman*.

She said, "I think you have the mum—mum—" She could hardly say it without keeling over with hilarity. "Mumps!" Ha, ha, hahahahahaha.

That was on a Tuesday. I watched TV. Ads for Taco Bell made my mouth water, painfully, enticing my salivary glands to burn through the inflammation. I drank fluids. I rested. Nic brought by my homework. I fought the low fever and was back in school by Monday. That's the short story of My Mumps Saga, humorous prequel to The Chicken Pox Chronicles.

After triumphing over the mumps, my stomach remained a scribble of pain. I was always nervous. So uptight and on edge that any tickle in my throat, any deep laugh from my belly, and I would start to cough. And cough. And cough until I would politely dry-heave my pain and nerves and confusion into the nearest garbage can, cafeteria tray, napkin, wastepaper basket, while Nic nonchalantly held my hair. Charming. I wasn't dying. I was just having my own version of a breakdown. I didn't talk about it with my parents. They were busy, what with their marriage deteriorating and all. Matt was beginning to get a little concerned, but I didn't make a big deal out of it, because what could he really do to help me? Nic? She was there for me, sure, but why clutter her day-to-day with the gory details of my emotional collapse? Guidance counselor? Face it, they respond only to anorexics, suicidals, and the Harvard-bound. If it weren't for Sylvia Plath, Matt's hunger for me, and my poetry, who knows where I would be? Would it be worse than where I am now?

Whatev. I got the chicken pox. I'm surprised no one called social services. My life is practically medieval. Appalachian. Pathetic. I need a guided meditation for "Building a Radiant Aura While Your Heart Folds in on Itself Like a Black Hole."

Am I being melodramatic? Probably. But it hurts so much, my parents splitting up. The reality of it. I am, everyday here in Poxville, trying to keep myself propped up with stupid jokes and stupid typing humor and The Bell Jar so I don't have to think about my mom and my dad.

Staying obsessed with The Bell Jar helps me keep all this tragedy in perspective. Reading for me is like a hot bath for Esther Greenwood. Getting all emotionally wrapped up in made-up people's lives gives me a chance to take a break from my own life, to stretch my legs under warm water, close my eyes, and inhale until I can think straight. I'm also trying to learn exactly how Esther does it, makes it through— New York, the suburbs, the asylum, Buddy—what tools does she use to endure it all?

My parents took turns reading to me before bed until I was practically thirteen. We did all of Harry Potter. Two chapters from Dad. Two chapters from Mom. When they went to bed, I'd turn on my bedside lamp and read chapter after chapter ahead until I passed out. But I loved listening to them, each in their own weird way telling me what happened next. Mom was all dramatic books-on-tape with it, and my dad was more straightforward. He just read it, and that was great too.

When Dad was driving me crazy, I could complain to Mom, mutter how that man of ours is infuriating but don't we love him anyway. And when Mom was totally pissing me off, I could tell Dad and he'd say something like, "Yeah, well, give her some space, and here, help me fold this laundry." Now I can't talk with either of them about the other one or anything. It's Mom. It's Dad. It's me. Each of our hearts are breaking and we can't even talk to one another like people do in normal families.

Now I have to have a "relationship" with each of them, totally independent of the other. Which is way more difficult. Especially *when you are an only child*. I have no one to share this with, no "Can you believe them, Chip? Let's get out of here, go for a bike ride in the forest preserves." There should be a rule that if you have only one child, you cannot split up—unless the said child dies, which would also be horrible.

What I'm trying to say is that my parents' divorce is one of the saddest things, and I can't believe it's happening to me. Although I act like I'm all mockety mock mock, and snarkity snark snark, I want my parents to be married. But my dad couldn't keep it in his pants. And here we are.

The term is "heartbreak" because that is how it feels. Your heart, ripped apart like a steak torn in half. And all the while you are supposed to move forward with your own stupid high school life, and do your homework, and look at college brochures, and make crap with Nic for your Etsy shop, and try on prom dresses, and cheer your lungs out for your boyfriend at semifinals. All this while the organ that is keeping you alive is a hot mess, stretching and twisting itself in your chest like a zombie pushing himself out of a grave.

When I'm feeling numb and want to cry, these are the things I think about:

1. Their goofy wedding photo with the tux and the white lace. They look so ridiculously happy, I want to keek.
2. How I used to climb into bed with them in the morning when I was little and they would let me.
3. When they brought Coffee home from the shelter on Valentine's Day with a red bow around her neck.

I don't think of these memories often. I thought if I typed them up, it would take away some of their power, like how turning on the bedside lamp makes the monster under the bed disappear. But seeing them in black and white makes these events seem like the names in *Suburban Life* of people who have died. It only makes the death of my parents' marriage seem more real.

DATE: July 25
MOOD: Totally Betrayed. YET AGAIN.
BODY TEMP: 101

When did my life become a total Lifetime movie cliché? I wouldn't really call these pages a "diary" or even a "journal." No hearts dotting the *I*s. They are just pages. Me, my brain, ink, and paper. Mine. Personal. It is obvious, and yet Gram feels that she must surreptitiously examine them while her pox-afflicted granddaughter sleeps like a log beneath the incapacitating coverlet.

On cable, mothers are always sneaking off and reading their daughters' diaries. They are looking for information about their sex lives. How far have they gone? In the really good movies, the daughter is a prostitute or a drug addict and/or sleeping with her history teacher, and there is a lot of screaming, and at some point the violated daughter stands and says, "How dare you!" or "You had no right!" Then the mother says, "Listen to me, young lady" or "As long as you're living under my roof." Don't get me wrong, it's a great script, but when it actually happens to you, it is sort of devastating.

Maybe I'm jumping to conclusions. All Gram said yesterday was, "They look nothing like fleabites" as she inspected my arm. It got cold in the center of my stomach—dread, I guess. Then she added, "I've heard people say they look like, ah, bug bites, you know? How about a cup of tea?"

I've been leaving my pages facedown on the bottom shelf of the nightstand. It's not like it's a big secret that I'm working on something in here. Typewriters are loud. My pages aren't bound in a Hello Kitty embossed pink leatherette diary complete with miniature key. But for Christ's sake, give me a freaking break. The pages are facedown for a reason. Can't we all be mature adults here? When chicken pox sleep takes over my body, it is the severely deep, drooling rest of the dead. Gram could move furniture and rip walls down around me, and I wouldn't wake up. Asleep, I am entirely vulnerable. I feel creeped out and under surveillance, like Sylvia did in the hospital with the tulips leering at her from the bedside table.

Curiosity killed the cat, Gram.

I thought we were friends.

Haven't I been betrayed enough?

Now I'll need to keep my pages under my pillow or between the mattress and box spring or like, on microfilm that I conceal in a false molar.

When I was maybe eight or nine, I spent a weekend at Gram's. She babysat me while my parents went away for a weekend. Wisconsin? Canada? Who knows. Who cares. All I remember is watching five straight hours of a *Tom and Jerry* cartoon marathon and whatever else bounced onto the screen when I hit the channel change buttons. Gram let me eat whatever I wanted. And what I wanted was BLTs. And Klondike bars. I was a chubby kid, and my parents were always pushing "healthy" snacks, such as baby carrots and hummus. Crunchy delicious apples. Roasted nuts rich in omega-3s. Sitting still and eating sandwich, after mayonnaise-laden sandwich, and square after square of creamy vanilla foil-wrapped treats while lush and violent cartoons kept me company is still an awesome memory. And not because of the sandwiches. But because Gram let me. Whatever I did was cool with her. I think of that, and *now*, at my moment of highest despair, she can't be trusted? Sigh. I think of eating now, and my stomach turns in disgust. My triceps are cramping up from all this typing. I don't think I have ever felt so alone as I do right now. This second. Like I am in a space pod orbiting the moon.

And when you knock on my door, Gram, and I don't answer, it is because I'm weak and weary, and crying so hard my ribs hurt, and honestly, I don't want you to see me this way.

The following is a transcript (from memory) of the phone call I received at 11:20 p.m. central time last night. I was the only one awake, lying on the couch clicking through late news and the opening monologues of unfunny late-night talk shows, a blanket around my shoulders like the queen of England or a homeless person. Before we begin, let me just say that after this so-called conversation, I have discovered that the landline is a superior method of phone communication to the cellular variety. It's as clear as a bell with no dropping of calls and no static. The handset is a big comfortable thing to talk into that actually fits my ear. No wonder Gram won't get rid of it.

> **MOM:** Keek? Izzat you? (Do you like how I am conveying her sloppy drunkenness?)

> **ME:** Mom? Hi! How are you?

MOM: How are *you*? Itchy? Can you hear that beeping?

ME: No. I'm better. But you know. Sick still. I feel like crap. Is everything okay? It's kinda late here. (I could hear mariachi music in background.)

MOM: Shit. The time—it's only nine here. I juz wanna check in with you to tell you how much I love you and that Amanda's just a stupid kid and that you are the most un-stupid person I know. *hic* I think Auntie wants me to stay another week. The baby's lungs are making *hic* progress, but she's still yellow as a banana. I mean, my sister really needs me here longer, at least a little closer to her original due date. Izzat okay with you?

ME: Another *week*? Mom! What're you talking about? I really need you—

MOM: Ah! That's *my* cell battery beeping. *hic* Tell your dad I love him, just not—aw, hell. You are my baby, Keekie. You were the most beautiful baby I have ever *hic* seen. I've had about twelve Coronas with your uncle here at this burrito joint and *hic* I miss you, Keek.

ME: Mom?

MOM: Aurora's plumping up like a little pizza puff, though. Just a little more time, maybe a week, maybe more, until she comes *hic* home. 168 hours. You'll live. Hello? Are you there?

ME: Mom?

MOM: Are you there?

ME: Mom?

MOM: Karina, I—

ME: Mom?

And then nothing.

Here's the thing about my mother. She's always doing whatever the hell she wants. In many respects this is an amazing quality. The Saturday after I began pinking chunks of my hair, I came home way too late from a knee-shaking L session with Matt, and there she was, my mother, with a skinny *pink* braid snaking down the side of her head. She wasn't even that mad at me for blowing my curfew.

"I'm fighting the gray, Keek. Besides, what's the point of being your own boss if you can't have a little antiestablishment fun with your hair?" Mom's hands were all pink, like she'd been juicing beets all night. Gloves, according to my mother, are for sissies. As are umbrellas, the AAA motor club, and paying retail. I'm glad she had her fun. But she had used up the last of the jar of Fuchsia Shock, so I had to order more and wait a week for delivery.

My mom *is* fun, okay? She is sofa king fun that I hardly even needed friends until I was twelve because we always knew how to have a good time together. We totally get each other and, if pressed, could probably telepathically communicate and win big money in Vegas. But she is also too much fun sometimes.

In books and on TV and in the movies, there are mothers who wear turtleneck sweaters, curl up with a cup of Celestial Seasonings herbal tea, and ask their daughters about their days. "How was school? What would you like for dinner? I've noticed that you have begun dyeing your hair interesting colors. Is anything bothering you, darling?"

And as exhibit B there is my dear mother, borrowing my Light My Sapphire nail polish and dragging out her old bass guitar to strum along to the nineties grunge crap playing in her earbuds. I know she is going through her own stuff now, but so? Priorities, people.

Lately Mom is the kid, the one who needs a stern talking to, perhaps an earlier curfew, and a trip to the school psychologist. It is not only infuriating, but also entirely confusing. Sometimes my mom puts her head on *my* shoulder and snuggles in like the world's tallest toddler. It makes my head spin. My entire equilibrium is upended when my head is higher than hers, staring at the roots of her hair and the beads of mascara on the tips of her eyelashes. If I'm the one comforting her, who's going to reassure *me*? So when I am at the end of my effing rope here at Gram's and this is the bizarre truncated conversation I get from my beloved mother, I get all kinds of aggravated.

Everyone I know, even Matt—usually even me—thinks my mom is "cool." Which, I think, has been a goal of my mother's life, to seem cool to her teenage daughter's pals. When some parents try to do this, they appear ridiculous. They wear foolish clothing and use nonsensical slang and are so permissive that before you know it, the boyfriends are sleeping over in the daughters' beds like in European art films. My mom is, however, authentically and for real *cool*. She has a badass wardrobe, talks tough, and often mentions how when she closes her eyes, she forgets she is old and a wife and a mother and not the lithe, fearless seventeen-year-old she meditates herself into believing she is.

Usually I love this about her, that she is but a wrinkle in time away from being exactly like me. Lately I do not. I want concerned. I want wise. Stable. There for me when things go ape-shit all over the place, someone to tell me *no* when I'm saying *yes* to everything because it feels like it's the fastest way to grow up and get through this. I want to be first. Before the Dine & Dash, before her marriage, before her stupid and selfish "trajectory." I'm hardly even on her to-do list.

Maybe it's like on airplanes when they tell you to fasten your oxygen mask before strapping it on to your own asphyxiating child. Maybe she needs to take care of her own shit before she can help me. I know, I know, I know. But still. I need to breathe too. She is so egomaniacal, my hands are itchy with rage, and no matter what I do, I can't catch my breath.

So when my mother started to talk about what a beautiful baby I was, I disappeared. I haven't been a baby for a hundred years. Babies can't talk. Can't text. Can't write anagrams in their sleep. Babies can't see you for the sham you are, and that's why she always—and I mean *always*—brings up the beautiful baby song and dance when she knows she is screwing up royally.

I just want her home. Is it so wrong for a sick girl to want her mother? They say that on the battlefield—France, Germany, Iraq—in the quiet dawn after a cease-fire, all you can hear are grown marines whimpering for their mothers, squealing into the morning mist like infant animals. So, yeah. I want my mom. Hell, I'd even take my dad at this point.

I know, I know. I'm always going on about wanting my space, and now that I have space, I want to be surrounded by people and streamers and bossa nova music like the host of a 1950s cocktail party of Plathian proportions. I want to be having a fabulous time, twirling my drink's umbrella between my thumb and forefinger, dozens of people hanging on my every word, asking me how I feel. And caring, deeply, what the answer is.

DATE: July 27
MOOD: Dressed, At Least
BODY TEMP: 101

No response to my business letter. Even though he's a wrestler, Matt can be a wuss. I lie here, sipping iced tea from a glass with hunting scenes painted on it. I'm dressed, sort of. I mean, I wouldn't go out in this ensemble, but it works for a housebound pox victim on the mend. Hair in a clip, T-shirt, bra, and underwear, totally comfy flowy jersey miniskirt. Flip-flops. Pox hither and thither on my so-white-it's-blue skin. I don't usually miss Matt like this, but today, because I am feeling better, because Gram's out food shopping, because my adulterous father is meeting with the soda syrup rep and Vienna meat distributor (thanks for the Post-it note, Dad), I feel so lonely I could die.

My addiction to <u>The Bell Jar</u> is interconnected with everything else going on with me of late. It is a work of great emotion and drama, and so is the Great Dine & Dash Divorce. And so is My Life. It's not so much that I identify with Esther (though I do). I just appreciate the way she sees the world. The ways she describes things, the things she finds funny, the ridiculous situations she gets herself into. Having this quasi-fictional character around all the time is comforting. She's not an invisible friend. It's more like she is living in a dollhouse in my brain. She is eating raw hamburger, breaking up with Buddy, playing with mercury on her bed at the asylum, working on her poems, all in the frontal lobe of my own head. Her entire existence is trying to figure out what her life is supposed to be while her heart breaks a little bit every day over the tragedy of being alive. And the writing is inspiring. I read The Bell Jar and I feel less alone. I feel smart. I feel like I have total permission to be as much of a smart-ass as Esther is because being a smart-ass is always preferable to being a dumb-ass. And to be entirely honest with myself, I don't always understand the poetry. Or parts of The Bell Jar. Or Sylvia Plath in general. But that is what is appealing to me! I don't understand most of what goes on in my own family, often in my own heart.

Speaking of the genius within, Gram hasn't mentioned anything remotely related to my pages recently, which is great news. Superb. I wanted to fake her out, plant big red herrings about my crystal meth addiction and penpal boyfriend in prison, but the real things that are happening in my actual life are disturbing enough. I never thought that the mundane hurts and betrayals of family and friends would be ten times more life-changing and gut-wrenching than dramatic made-up situations in fiction. Nothing is as it seems in my life anyway. Everything feels surreal. Mom's call really freaked me out the other night. As if I don't have enough to worry about, now I'm adding alcoholism and child abandonment to the list.

Being locked away with the chicken pox isn't helping matters. I haven't been outside in days. I have been kidnapped and held in an undisclosed location. When I'm not typing (and sometimes even when I am), I feel like I am underwater, trudging along the bottom of the ocean in weighted boots while Judge Judy, typewriters, and babies in jars float past my diver's mask, as elusive and ephemeral as jellyfish. I feel like everyone who is supposed to care about me—Mom, Dad, Gram, Nic, even Matt—are all on the surface, not looking deep enough to find me. Maybe when I come up for air, it will turn out that I don't really have chicken pox, Dad didn't really sleep with Amanda, Mom isn't really in California, Matt really is the person I thought he was when we met. And Aurora? She doesn't even exist. Ha. Ha. Ha. It's all been an elaborate mermaid dream. How about we turn your tail into legs and just get on with it?

I'm feeling better, anyway.

Although the coverlet still feels like it will smash my lungs to my spine if I don't keep it off me, I think the fever's coming down, because my hair has stopped hurting. Never fear. I still feel like typing. About nothing and everything. Matt mostly, today. I didn't dream about him last night as much as I thought of him during the day, between naps, egg salad sandwiches, and JJ. I thought of him, dreamily. When Matt and I are alone on the L-shaped couch, there is nothing else. No family, no D&D, no school, or even time. This voice in my brain that is, essentially, *me*, and talks all the freaking time? It is blissfully silent as Matt flutters his hands across my stomach and up the insides of my thighs, making me shiver. He smells like Downy fabric softener and sometimes tastes like it too. For the record, I don't use softener. It is made with animal fat. That's part of what gives it its softening effect. I don't like the idea of—basically butter—clinging to my clothes or towels, but I love it on Matt. He smells like clean comfort and tastes like flowers, mint, and salt. His arms are hard, his hips and thighs solid with muscle, mouth hot, tongue alive, and all I want is wanting when we are in the darkness in the L.

When we're on the L, he stares straight through to my center, his mouth half-open, pupils dilated. I am his drug. His must-have, surrender or die. He is so hard against my thigh I can feel the pulse in his lap through the denim. And when he whispers "You are so beautiful," I want him to bite right through my neck as we rub against each other, wet feral creatures.

That was just for you, Gram.

The thing is, we never really get much further than that. Although I do not want to die a virgin, I'm not quite ready to not be one anymore. Despite everything, Matt's very polite about my virginity situation. Sometime he treats me like a burn victim, like he doesn't want to touch me too much because something might sting or ooze or get sticky (!). Having said that, he totally knows how far he can push me without pissing me off. Or, before I freak out. Which are usually the same thing.

When you are Dorothy and the rest of your life is the tornado, the last thing you want to do is add lost virginity to the mix. For real. But if I were looking for the perfect candidate for my historic deflowering, it would be Matt. His beautiful face and body are merely a bonus to the amazing guy he is on the inside.

Have I mentioned that he makes dinner once a week for his family? And not just mac 'n' cheese and frozen pizzas, but roasted chickens. Mashed potatoes. Sautéed spinach with garlic. And they light a candle and all sit and eat dinner together. I'm not even kidding.

Once, I helped Matt make a family dinner of potato

curry from a recipe I found online. We chopped and stirred and set the table, and sometimes it felt like we were little kids playing house, and other times it felt like we were totally married. And I loved it. We sat there by candlelight, talking about The Scarlet Letter and A Tale of Two Cities with his parents while I held Matt's hand under the table. I haven't felt that safe or calm since before my parents started the restaurant. The potato curry was definitely missing some important ingredient we must have forgotten, but Matt went on and on about how delicious and amazing it was, and just thinking about it now is making me burn up with love. I should just look past any and all of his faults and love him to pieces. Oh, but for the virginity.

I'm as neurotic as Esther Greenwood when it comes to this particular subject. I want to be both a virgin and a nonvirgin at the same time. Which is impossible. Just because I don't want to "lose" my "virginity" doesn't mean I wouldn't mind misplacing it for a while. It's exhausting, this always thinking about it and wondering about it so it becomes this great fulcrum of my existence. But much to my chagrin, that's exactly what's happening.

Even Esther saw the world as being split into people who had done it and people who hadn't. She imagined that once she slept with someone, she would transform in an invisible yet spectacular way. And for some girls, I think this is true. The Monday after the weekend of the senior formal, some girls seemed more alive than the others. They tossed the hair from their eyes in a new, knowing, and glamorous way. They even rotated the combinations at their lockers with a new sensuousness that to me indicated that over the weekend they had happily abandoned their virginity at the side of the road. It was *obvious* that there was absolutely a before and an after.

Anyway, I've seen Matt's penis before, Gram. And I use the word "penis" because that is what it looked like. There are really no better words to describe it.

It wasn't like I woke up that morning, looked at the calendar, and thought, *Hmm what a fantastic day to take a good long look at my boyfriend's nakedness.* That whole Saturday was weird. Raining and humid. The streets smelled like wet puppy, and the air seemed to press against my skin, making me languid and tired. Matt's parents were away for the day. I didn't have much going on, aside from pulling all the Post-it notes from my copy of The Bell Jar so when I read it again it would be with fresh eyes.

Usually when he called, I'd tell Matt to meet me at the D&D because there was free food. There's an old Centipede video game in the corner. And there were no beds. The only door you could close was the freezer. But Amanda and Dad had already been in there, contaminating the cheese with their illicit lust, so when Matt asked if I wanted to come over, what was I going to say—no?

Being in his house, just the two of us, was beginning to feel wrong and exciting, how I imagine shoplifting must feel. It was the same way I felt fake smoking with Amanda, reading <u>The Bell Jar</u> in algebra class, or eating spoonfuls of mayonnaise from the giant jar. At Matt's house there were big melted glass sculptures and copper cowboys swinging lassos in a giant oak bookcase. There were stainless steel appliances in the kitchen, which made it feel different from our house. Fancier and bigger and just overall a lot nicer. But more than that, it seemed more solid than our house. Half its contents were not about to be put inside a U-Haul and dragged away against their will. Everything, everyone, belonged there. I felt like a total intruder.

Up in Matt's room I sat on the edge of his unmade bed and leaned back as nonchalantly as I could, considering. The very smell of him emanating from his sheets made my breath quicken. Matt stood between my knees, bumping them farther apart with his khaki-covered thighs. And then he leaned forward and said, "Hi, Keek," before doing that thing where he nuzzles his nose under mine till he finds the very center of my mouth and then goes in for the kill. As he was kissing me, he ran his finger from my earlobe down the front of my black T-shirt, bouncing over a nipple like it was a speed bump, and kept going down to my navel until I was practically panting. He stood up, his mouth hanging open a little, a slight bulge in his pants.

"Wanna see it?" Matt asked, breathless, and I was all, *Oh, really?* But I looked at him and said, "Well, all right, sure, I guess," which is almost *exactly* what Esther said in a similar situation. Life imitating art, or what?

Before I knew it or could change my mind, Matt practically ran toward this empty-looking fish tank. My darling boyfriend rustled some leaves, lifted a piece of bark, gently cupped *something* between his hands, and walked toward the bed, where I was sitting, as prim and innocent as Miss-freaking-Muffet. Matt opened his hands as if opening a book, and there, sitting in his palms like a beating heart, was a—tarantula. The spider was the size of an iPhone. With fur. And eyes. And fangs. And then I was wishing it *was* his stupid penis, because that would have freaked me out sofa king less.

Despite my interest in eco-chic living and my high regard for the animal kingdom, my whole being wanted to leap up and grab the nearest broom, hockey stick, or rolled-up *Wrestling USA* magazine and squash it into a furry bloody mess before it killed us all. I could only think of it leaping onto my face and paralyzing me with venom so that I couldn't even scream, "You fool! Run for your life!" But I just sat there, waiting to see what Matt was going to do with the spider.

Matt put one hand in front of the other, hand over hand, climbing across the bed so the spider could use him as a stepping-stone to get closer to, er, me. "I just got him.

His name's Hogan. Like Hulk Hogan? That old pro wrestler? Is he awesome or what?" Slow and cautious, the spider seemed desperate for Matt's hands to guide it to safety.

"Here," he said. "Pet him. He feels amazing." Its fur was a silvery-orange color, and up close it looked stupid and vulnerable, a tourist downtown asking directions.

"Come on, Karina. Just be nice to him, okay?"

O-freaking-K. And to be nice, because I felt sorry for the thing and even sorrier for Matt, the boy who loved a spider, I gingerly put one finger—recently painted with Blue My Mind, the last nail polish I'd bought with Amanda—onto its back and petted it. It was warmish. And soft. And although I could not feel its heartbeat, per se, it was alive and it seemed to like me.

"Here." Matt pulled my hand out so the tarantula could walk on it. And I let it. I let the spider slowly tiptoe over my trembling hand with my dark blue nails, and it looked like a photo on a CD cover. I found myself offering it my other hand, and then the other as Matt had. It walked all over me for about a minute as if we were a long-standing vaudeville act. Keek and Hogan, ladies and gentlemen!

Matt? He just stood there watching us, smiling like crazy. It tickled, the spider, terrifying and mesmerizing me at the same time. Then Matt scooped up Hogan and we gently placed him back in the fish tank with the bark and moss. Home sweet home. We held spider-germ-covered hands as we walked back to the bed without talking.

I took hold of a belt loop while Matt slid his hand up my shirt, walking his fingers Hogan-style up toward the clasp of my bra. I stood on my toes, arching my back so our pelvises could touch as we kissed. While I was thinking about what I could do next to him, Matt somehow maneuvered his other hand to take the rubber band out of my pony tail, freeing my hair in pink and black ribbons, down to my shoulders.

Remember when you were a little kid and some adult would come up to you and sweep your hair out from under your collar, and it felt so good and cool and it made you shudder with delight? This is what Matt was making me feel. New. And brave and so good that my body. Was. Not. Listening. To. Me. My hands became the hands of some kind of Victorian libertine—aka, total horndog—and before my intelligence or my fear of pregnancy, heartbreak, and disappointment could intervene, those same hands that had just tangoed with a tarantula were fiddling with his belt buckle. Fearless.

Matt grabbed my wrists. "Are you sure you want to do this?" And I didn't even *know* what THIS was, but still, I nodded and licked my lips. We were going to have our first times together, and this could have been it but not if he kept talking.

I have seen Matt wrestle, and he is fierce and so heavy

that seniors can't even knock him over. So to make him quiver as my polished nails slid between his underwear and his hot skin was intoxicating.

And I was pulling his gray boxer-briefs down his hips, and there was all this hair! Straight hairs and then this, like, penis. Nestled in this dark hair nest like a defenseless blind baby bird. It was the most naked thing I have ever seen. As I looked at it, it grew before my very eyes, plumping and elongating, transforming into this thing with power and heat. I could see Matt's heartbeat in it. I wanted to protect it, wrap it in angora and cashmere, not drop on my knees or let it anywhere too near me.

When Esther first saw Buddy's penis, she thought of poultry parts—particularly neck and gizzards—and was totally disheartened. I totally remembered this there in Matt's room, and it was so identical to my own feelings that I could hardly stand it. This is the thing about great literature. It reads like truth and sticks to you forever and lets you know that you are not alone.

That's when I pulled Matt's underwear back up and over, careful not to bump or further agitate the throbbing beast, and said, "I gotta go." Not because I was disgusted or anything but because I was freaked out. And trembley. And embarrassed. It was just all too much.

Matt's pupils were big. "Come on, Karina. Don't I get to see you?"

And, um, no. Well.

"Come here," he whispered, and he hugged me and kissed me on the neck, like he understood that I was about to cry. You know those devices they sell on late-night TV that you put inside an egg to scramble it while it's inside the shell? I felt like the egg inside the shell. Every emotion in *Roget's Thesaurus*: shy, adventurous, ashamed, afire, terrified, enamored, invincible, vulnerable, happy, depressed, joyful, shocked. You name it, I was feeling it. The whole omelet, all scrambled up in the center of my guts, and it made me want to weep like a baby. So I sat on the bed, patient, letting Matt lift my shirt and gently pull down the bra cups and look at me, a little naked. He seemed impressed. Quiet with awe. And *that* made me want to cry. And then he knelt over and put a nipple in his mouth, like the baby in the health class video, and *that* made me want to cry. His tongue flicks sent thrills down to my groin and back up that were so intense I thought I was going to dry-heave. This was when I stood and said, "Matt, I gotta go home," grabbed my bag, and escaped.

In The Bell Jar, when Esther Greenwood finally bites the bullet and gets rid of her virginity, she almost bleeds to death. Unbeknownst to her, she has this rare condition and she almost dies. This sounds like something overprotective parents would make up to scare the crap out of their virgin daughters. Could this happen to me? Not likely. But it is an excellent metaphor for the power of virginity. It's not leaving without a fight.

I'm sure if I started to bleed to death, Matt wouldn't dump me in the doorway of the nearest ER and head for the hills like Esther's deflowerer. Matt is, in most regards, a gentleman. Besides, who knows if Matt is even still my boyfriend? Hours before I got seriously sick, we had this vicious fight and I'm sure he thinks of me as an inexperienced idiot with a virginity hang-up. I'm the black and pink Plath-loving freak show that is more than he can handle with his junior year coming up, and all.

After I told Amanda (Why *Amanda*? Why not Nicola? Or even MY MOTHER?) about the tarantula, the penis, the escape, she said, "God, you are such a tease." But now that I've had a couple of feverish weeks to reflect on things, I'm like, Tease *this*. Teasing is taunting a boy with the promise of sex in order to manipulate him, and then not going through with it. Which is *so* not what I was doing. I'm not taunting anybody with anything. I'm making this up as I go along. I want things to feel right, and the more I mess around with Matt, the more right it feels and when it starts to feel wrong for me, we stop.

Why was Amanda trying to make me feel like crap about it? That was a red flag right there. She wasn't on my side. It would never occur to her to help me through this, to help me make sense of it, to explain to me how to prepare emotionally for when I actually go through with it. She was on her own side. On experience's side and rubbing that in my face like I was a naughty puppy that had an accident on the living room carpet. Right then and there I should have done what Esther did with Doreen: decide to have nothing to do with her. Shoulda, woulda, coulda.

Speaking of heartbreak, *oh, why isn't Matt desperately looking for me?* Maybe he's scared. Maybe he's at the gym, doing a thousand sit-ups a day trying to forget about me. Maybe he just doesn't care. But there should be LOST signs on telephone poles, a homing pigeon lookout station, a phone tree with Gram's number at the end of it. He could have at least popped his head into the D&D for two seconds. Jorge could have updated him. The address is on the business letter!

I am *here*. I have hardly moved for a week!

The world is coming to an end. Have you heard? In a hundred years there will be no more oceans. There will be no grass, clouds, or cures for all the diseases unleashed by the environment. All the coats, scarves, mittens, and waterproof boots often used in what was once known as "winter" will be better utilized making huts and teepees to shield us from the thousand degree sun in January. I mock, and yet I am terrified. This is a world full of horrible death and destruction. Breast cancer. Premature babies. Terrorists. Oil spills. Nuclear bombs. The Apocalypse. And what am I most upset about? My parents. Splitting up.

How noble.

Still.

People get divorced every damn day. JJ has exes on her show every night who can't agree who gets the dog, who gets the car, whose fault it is that the taxes on their trailer lot weren't paid last year. Five out of ten marriages end in divorce. I'm no math star, but that is half—50 percent. Even at school you can't throw a rock without hitting some kid who is off to dad's for the weekend. But it is not happening to just anyone. It is happening to me.

The night Dad moved out was surreal. I was lying on my bed, listening to the house. Coffee was at my feet breathing with the regularity of a life support machine in a hospital drama. The rest of the house was so silent, I heard my parents' marriage die, the house icy still as the spirit of what I once knew as "my parents" floated into the ether.

And just as I felt as demoralized as I have ever felt, who walks into my room in a corduroy jacket carrying a crappy vinyl suitcase, but my father. He sat on my bed. I will never forget seeing his tears running into his stubble. It was right up there with my first French kiss with Matt outside the cafeteria and the chicken pox blood bath with Gram. My dad crying. I saw him cry, once, at the end of some war movie on HBO. But that wasn't even real crying. It was, like, oh-there-must-be-something-in-my-eye wetness.

It was only about four months ago, but I don't really remember what he said. I think it was something like, "I'm sorry." Was there a light on? There must have been. "You know your mom and I have been having some trouble." By this point Coffee had woken up, put her head on his knee, like, *Oh, beloved master, where are you going?*

"I don't know if or when I'll be back, but I'll see you this weekend. We'll do a movie or something." Coffee looked like she was about to kill herself with woe. "I'm staying at Gram's. You can call me there or on my cell. This is all really"—he moved his hands, gesturing in the air, searching for the right words, and then he let out a weird choking man-sob—"complicated."

I was stunned, okay? I hadn't realized it had come to this. No trial separation? No romantic getaway weekend to talk things out? What the hell is counseling for if you're going to break up and move out anyway?

I do remember, quite clearly, what I said to him. Now, this is my dad. My father. And he has been and always will be. He can be a real asshole, but I love him. I mean, he was crying on my bed and I wanted to throw my arms around his shoulders and tell him that everything was going to be okay. So what did I say? What were my loving words of wisdom and we'll-get-through-this-somehow comeback?

"What about the Dine & Dash?"

Because it's all about the restaurant. Always is. Over our rare sit-down dinners or family outings (Cubs game, Art Institute, Gram's for lasagna), talk would end up being about the D&D. Lunch specials, customer service, dishwasher repair, license renewal, dough paddles, pizza boxes, lunch specials, on and on and on. It had become the replacement for talking about anything else. Anything important. So at the lowest point of this whole debacle, when my insides felt like all my bones had collapsed into a heap in the pit of my being, what do I ask about? The freaking restaurant.

And he said, "It's open. We'll figure it out as we go along." Then, "I love you, Keek."

"I love you too," I muttered.

Then he picked up the suitcase and walked out of my bedroom with Coffee following him, and I didn't even cry. Not one teardrop.

Alone in my pathetic bedroom, it was quiet like after the credits of a movie, after the "no animals were harmed," "special thanks," and the logo for the production company, when the whole wall seems like it's still moving. Then a whimper, a low growl. Coffee? No. Mom. I pictured her in her bedroom, gnashing her teeth, her pillowcase soaked with snot and saline. But at that moment I didn't care.

There's this part in The Bell Jar, right before Esther leaves New York, when she starts to cry at a photo shoot because she feels disillusioned and weak and basically, a shell of herself. Which is how I felt about my parents' marriage. Everything was a discarded useless version of what it used to be. I knew things were not good with them for a long time, and yes, there was a little ping of recognition because their breakup proved my gut instincts had been right, but some important part of me climbed out of the house that night. My joy? My sense of security? My childhood, I guess. And what was left was me, feeling as weightless and insignificant as the skin shed by a snake.

I got up.

Even though it was after eleven at night, I ran a bath, as hot as I could stand. I closed the door and lowered myself in like a tea bag. My brain stopped thinking of anything except how to make a moment out of this, how to mark this night as the night I knew I would never be purely happy again. And when I say "purely" I mean just plain happy with no darkness beneath the glee, happy like little kids when they ride on carousels or blow out candles. Now I have the knowledge that the world is mostly a brutal place of treachery and heartbreak, where not even parents can keep it together. For Esther Greenwood, that moment was when her father died, but for me it was when mine left home.

When I raised my arms in the bath to push my hair out of the way, water dripped from my elbows like the tears that wouldn't come out of my eyes. When I was a kid, I pretended I was a mermaid in the tub. The faucet was an enchanted secret waterfall, the Suave shampoo a magical siren potion to enchant pirates and sailors. That night in the tub, I was just a girl, terrified of what would happen next. In the corner between tub and wall was a red and white striped can of shaving cream. Dad's. I pushed the top and covered the surface of the water with white foam until air came out of the nozzle and pushed the white out of the way.

It was too late to call Nic to talk, and what would I have said? "Please be my best friend again now that I really need you, even though I don't deserve it"? Or "I still love you. Please help me"? "I'm so sorry I always take you for granted"? "I miss you"?

Dad used to take Nic and me to the movies and roller-skating birthday parties, and we'd slept over at each other's houses every weekend for the previous four years. Before high school. Before Matt. Before Amanda. Before everything started to fall apart. We were like a superhero duo, figuring out the most fun and efficient ways to thwart our common enemy—boredom. With Nic I could always be myself. I didn't have to try to seem older, pretend to smoke, or think of new ways to avoid going too far. We could be in a room together and read without music on or anything. How many people can do *that* together? A rare few.

Nic's parents were nice people who loved each other so much, they had four kids together. Nic was the baby and had a whole tribe of siblings to keep her laughing and busy, to keep a bell jar from descending upon her. I just had me. And I was ashamed and alone, and I still can't call her. She probably doesn't even know that I have the chicken pox. One day someone will invent a device that will allow you to apologize without having to actually say anything.

Gram is home with fresh provisions.
Good thing too.
I'm sofa king starving.

DATE: July 29
MOOD: Indebted
BODY TEMP: 101

This morning I was typing and thinking. Thinking and typing beneath the hundred-pound coverlet. It is as heavy as a dead body, and using it is creeping me out. What is it made of? I was compelled to reveal its mystery. There are small wood buttons fastening the bottom of the duvet cover together. I unbuttoned them, one by one, and peeled the top back to reveal its innards. It is made of wool. Four wool blankets, one on top of the other, attached at the corners with big knots of orange yarn, the kind girls like my mom wore in their hair in the 1970s. Exhausted suddenly, I buttoned the outer cotton envelope and slid beneath it wearing my clothes. I shut my bruisy eyes and let the thing, now innocent and benign—yet still unnaturally heavy—crush me to the mattress.

I had been asleep ten minutes, an hour, the whole morning—who's to say?—when there was a polite knock on my door, and Gram popped her head in. "Rise and shine, doll face. You have some visitors."

Visitors? I was still a little asleep and kept saying *Vis-i-tors* in my head, like *Glad-i-a-tors*, and my stomach turned, like a yappy little dog doing a flip, because who would come to visit me? I am the girl that time forgot. I redid my ponytail, sprayed some ancient chartreuse-colored Muguet Des Bois cologne from my great-grandma's dresser onto my neck to mask any poxian funk, made sure my bra was on straight, and padded out to the living room.

"KEEK!"

"Neeeeee-co-laahhh!"

And we were hugging like chimpanzee sisters on the cover of a Hallmark card. As we put our arms around each other, I felt lighter, supported, and happy. I hadn't hugged Nic in forever. And it felt so great—like, normal. It was as if there had never been any weirdness between us, as if I had never chosen Matt or Amanda over her, not even once. Nic is no fool. She gets it. She was forgiving me without talking about it, because she simply wants me in her life as badly as I want her in mine. I guess that's true friendship in a nutshell.

So my face was over her shoulder and I was practically floating with happiness when who did I see, sitting in my grandma's upholstered chair, knee bouncing up and down like a sewing machine needle, but Earl the Squirrel. With the least amount of acne he has ever had. And a hickey. On his neck.

"Yo, Keek. You don't look as bad as Nic said you would." He gave me an embarrassed kind of smile. My eyes were bulging from my head, asking Nic, *What's with the Squirrel?* But she ignored the question.

"I just said to not recoil in horror," Nic said, "just in case you were totally covered in pox, or whatever. Which you are not. So, whew!"

Nic looked so cute. She wore this white sleeveless mod minidress with a mandarin collar and had all kinds of random plastic bracelets up her arm, like a kid playing dress-up in her mom's jewelry box. A good look, for sure. Her hair was shorter than I remembered, and as I tried to think of the last time we were actually in the same room together, all I could come up with was our last English final, before school let out. Which was hardly together. And was a long time ago.

"So, chicken pox, huh?" she said. Then she tossed herself down onto the couch and ran her fingers through her new short hair, her bracelets clacking with little bursts of applause.

"And Amanda. And my Dad. I don't know how much—"

"I saw yer dad at the D&D and heard whatever Matt's told Earl. So I'm up to speed. You can give me a detailed debriefing another time. You look kind of good, dahlink, considering."

Nic is a lot of things, but she is always honest, good, and down to earth (also nice to her mother), and I had a lot of forgiveness to beg from her. We never did not have fun together. It was her idea to open an Etsy shop selling brace-lets made by half-melting toothbrushes in boiling water that we then bent around our wrists. She was the one who encouraged me to test for honors English before high school started. She knew me when my parents were happy together and I thought divorce was a sad, destructive thing that other, more screwed-up people went through.

"So, um, what do you do all day here? Lose your mind?" Earl asked, and he wasn't half-kidding. "Oh, and sorry, but are you contagious, or what?" There was something different about him. Instead of the buzzing energy that usually made him seem like a walking ball of TV static, he was more, I don't know, still? Serene? I could actually see him, as if for the first time. He looked like Ichabod Crane, but in a good way, sitting in the chair with his pointy elbows and long legs all over the place, like a game of pick-up sticks. He wore baggy black linen shorts and a vintage bowling T-shirt with the name Stan embroidered over the pocket. Which I'm sure was a gift from Nic.

"No. I'm not contagious. But your parents probably had you vaccinated. Right?" This was the most I had ever said to him. "How're *you*?" And I looked straight at his ridicu-lous hickey and he turned twenty-five different shades of red/crimson/scarlet/vermilion/ruby.

"I'm pretty good," he said, and looked at Nic, then started blushing all over again. I didn't know how else to approach this. I didn't want to seem all desperate and needy, but if Nic and Earl could find me, surely that man of mine could too?

"So, hey. Have you heard from Matt or anything? I haven't, um, for a while, and my phone . . ." And kill me now that I even had to ask in the first place.

"You know, it's weird. I haven't really. I've been kind of, er, busy lately." Earl gave Nic this puppy-dog-in-love gaze, which was simultaneously cute and nauseating.

"Yeah, Earl and I have been garage sailing, Keek, and when you get better, you are so coming with us. It's been an amazing season."

Nic and I had been garage sailing—our own oh-so-clever term for it—since we were old enough to ride our bikes through the alleys. We talked about it with clenched teeth, like we were talking about yachting or cotillion at the country club.

Nic stood and spun and clacked her bracelets at me. "Score, right?" Meaning her outfit in its adorable entirety cost less than ten dollars.

Last summer, before high school started, we would get a *Suburban Life* newspaper and a red Sharpie and circle the most promising sale events, mapping out our route and filling our handlebar baskets with crap we could not live without. Record albums and fondue paraphernalia, dresses, jackets, square-toed patent leather boots. Cocktail rings, Adam Ant posters, fish tank toys, and giant daisy pins. How we loved the ephemera of suburban living, repurposed with knowing worldliness for our own lives, making everything we did seem unique and full of unearned gravitas because the very objects themselves had a history separate from our own.

I get all loquacious thinking about vintage crap.

"Here, Keek." Earl stood up, a gallant skeleton, and handed me a brown box with a blue bow on it. "We got you a present." Then he went over to sit next to Nic and *held her hand.* And all of a sudden I loved them both so much, I got dizzy.

"For real?" I said, because here were two people I had not been especially nice to, particularly of late. And they were giving me a gift. I so desperately needed someone to be nice to me for no good reason that I didn't even need to open the stupid box. They could have given me a rock they'd found in the alley, and I would have loved it.

Dear reader, it was not a rock.

It was a book.

And not just any book. It was—

Are you sitting down?

The.

Bell.

Jar.

A 1966 Faber and Faber hardcover edition with black-and-white concentric circles on the *intact* dust jacket! A collector's item if ever there was one. I had to grab on to the armrest on the wingback chair so I wouldn't fall over. I squealed like a maniacal porpoise with delight.

"Got it in Berwyn," the Squirrel said.

"For one dollar!" Nic screamed, and we spontaneously high-fived while the Squirrel gave a giggle-snort out of his nose. "I just knew you would love it to death," Nic said, and we were all laughing and happy. Then the Squirrel had to "take a leak," so I pointed the way to the bathroom.

As soon as he was out of earshot, Nic put a hand in my face in a talk-to-the-hand gesture and dramatically pulled one half of her mandarin collar down to reveal a hickey of her own—the size and color of a flattened penny souvenir from the Sears Tower.

!!

And then she said, "Before you say anything, he is Awe. Some. And really funny. And we have so much fun together. And holy crap, Earl-the-freaking-Squirrel is my boyfriend." She looked drunk, she was so giddy with happiness. And then the Squirrel came out with his long hands wet from washing them. (I think he was afraid of catching the pox from my towels.) Nic and I stopped giggling and being best friends. And then suddenly it dawned on me that if Nic were Esther, I would have been *her* Doreen, with my selfish, quasi-slutty, and rude behavior. And I guess this is how it is. One man's meat is another man's poison and all that. Obviously the rest of the world doesn't stop when yours crashes to the ground. I'm happy—for the both of them, really.

It's just—

I felt as demoralized as Esther watching Doreen dance with the cowboy, knowing they were growing more and more in love with each other by the second while I sat there all alone, scratching the one remaining pox on my ankle into oblivion. And if Matt and the Squirrel start to talk about us and compare notes about us, Nic and me, and share how far they've gone and whatever, I will happily spend the rest of my days in the Cook County juvenile detention center without parole for a double homicide. But then I look at the Squirrel, and he's cool. He looks scared and quiet and more like a decent fellow than I have ever seen him. And Nic? She looks like the cover of freaking *Seventeen* magazine, she is so pink-cheeked, fashionable, and self-assured.

I, however, look like something the proverbial cat dragged in.

Miaow.

(Which is how Sylvia spells "meow" in <u>The Bell Jar</u>, Faber and Faber edition, 1966).

I am feeling so much better today that I actually feel like eating. I am not a vegetarian, but one day I would like to be one. I can totally eat meat formed into other shapes, like chicken nuggets, hamburger patties, hot dogs, fish sticks, etc. It's when the meat is just, like, *meat* that I have a hard time with it. The chicken leg, the T-bone steak, the salmon fillet, all look like they were just on the actual animal a minute ago, helping them walk, graze, swim, whatever.

Besides, someone has to offset the D&D's industrially slaughtered cow consumption. We provide prepared meats of all kinds to half the Chicago suburbs. Free delivery. I can't wash my hands of it if it's paying for college, now, can I? Gram has been very supportive, what with the egg salad sandwiches and such. And I really appreciate that.

She also brought all the ingredients I requested for my recipe festival and is going to look in the basement for some of her old Fiestaware and Corelle and teacups she got as wedding gifts. For the remainder of my incarceration/recovery/breakdown, I am going to prepare food items from The Bell Jar and report my findings. I will eat what Esther ate. I will consume the foods of the 1950s with glee and a sense of adventure.

It's something to do.

Gram said the store carried only eight cans of Spam.

She is totally apologizing for invading my privacy by reading my pages.

If The Bell Jar has taught me anything, it is that everyone, no matter how seemingly normal, put together, and successful, is complicated. Everyone has lived through traumatic life events that you would never guess just by looking at them. Which is comforting to know as you go through your own screwed-up stuff. This was never truer for anyone than for my gram. We had a total girl extravaganza yesterday, complete with tea drinking, chitchatting, and the trying on of vintage dresses.

All she had to say was, "I have a bunch of old clothes in the guest bedroom you might get a kick out of," and I was down the hall and in front of the closet door, as perky as one of Santa's elves. At first I thought it was going to be clothes from a few years ago or, be still my heart, the 1980s. But when I opened the door, I saw cotton belted dresses, beaded cardigans, cigarette pants. Clothes from the 1950s. Some were Gram's and some were her mom's, and most were still in dry cleaner bags. I had to sit down on the carpet—SO I WOULDN'T FAINT.

The recipe festival would have to wait.

As Gram pulled out each garment, she told a little story about wearing it, which was hilarious and weird and inspiring. It was like I was on the sidewalk in front of the Amazon Hotel and Esther Greenwood was in her room tossing her city clothes out the window and I was catching them in my outstretched arms, one by one, as they fluttered down. Some items were a little worn, but some looked brand new. Most of them—miracle of miracles— fit me. Or would when I wrapped a black studded belt around my waist a few times. On the top shelf were round boxes that contained hats with veils and churchy head covers with webs of daisies. A box on the floor was a treasure chest of melamine bracelets. But my favorite by far is a sea foam green beaded cardigan with white pearls and rhinestones along the collar. It doesn't have buttons but a tiny hook at the top to keep it shut. Thanks to my constant fever and constant air-conditioning, I am more than comfortable wearing it around the house. Plathware.

So we were talking and laughing, and Gram was spraying us both with Muguet Des Bois cologne and pulling out scatter pins from the back of her jewelry box and pinning them to my T-shirt, and I was having the time of my life, learning all kinds of things about her that even my own mother and father probably didn't know. Information that made Gram (even more) amazing to me, knowledge that I wouldn't have been able to handle before this summer. Here's the lowdown, in no particular order:

1. She was madly in love with someone. He died in a car crash. Totally distraught and heartbroken, she married his best friend, who happened to be a real jerk.
2. She was a cub reporter for the *Chicago Tribune* in the 1950s. She covered premieres at movie theaters downtown and interviewed the celebrities who attended.
3. The first person she interviewed was Tab Hunter, and she was so starstruck that she couldn't ask him anything except, "What is your favorite color?" and "Do you prefer blue- or brown-eyed girls?" At the time no one knew that he was gay.
4. Later she was a stenographer at the Chicago supreme court and recorded a lot of depressing and bizarre cases.
5. She had what was known as a "nervous breakdown" when my dad went off to college. Shock treatment, injected sedatives, the whole Bell Jar.

I KNOW!!!!!
!
!
!
!
!

FOUR HAIKUS FROM GRAM'S CLOSET

GREEN GINGHAM DRESS WITH
BRASS KNOT BUTTONS, 1952

Sweet sixteen party,
Sipped root beer floats through long straws,
And called them black cows.

LINEN DRESS WITH PETER PAN COLLAR
AND BLACK BOW, 1956

First job interview,

Took personality test.

The best job ever!

PURPLE AND GOLD PLAID
DRIVING COAT, 1957

First date with true love.
Fed zoo animals corn, months
Before the car crash.

STRAPLESS BLACK SILK DRESS WITH DEEP KICK PLEAT, 1958

Its plunging neckline
Showed creamy décolletage.
Mother hated it.

DATE: July 31
MOOD: Ravenous
BODY TEMP: 101.1 (which is also a great radio station!)

When I packed to come here, I threw enough crap into a bag to get me through a week because I wasn't planning on an extended stay. I didn't even bring my iPod. Now laundry must be done, and so, I am doing it. Laundry is something I like to do. It is very straightforward. Toss it in. Add soap. Wait. Remove. Dry. Fold. When the clothes come out of the dryer, they don't even smell like you anymore, so it's like they are brand new. At home I like to use eco-friendly dryer balls or lavender sachets instead of dryer sheets. But I am a stranger in a strange land. I make do.

Gram's basement is low ceilinged. The basement has its own entrance from the driveway, a sitting room with a bookcase and an easy chair, a closet, and a bedroom with its own bathroom. That is Dad's room—aka Quasimodo's Lair. The rest of the basement is unfinished and that's where the washing machine and dryer are.

I have to pass Dad's room to get to the machines, and I hold my breath as I walk past it because it is so intimate and humiliating to see what he has been reduced to. When my parents were trying to fix things in counseling, I thought, *Well, if they did break up, maybe it wouldn't be so bad.* I imagined my dad would get his own apartment in the city with an amazing view of Lake Michigan and stereo system and a maid service. This bunker is beyond my comprehension.

I'm feeling better but still pretty weak. I pop my clothes in and lean against the washer, suddenly exhausted. The basement is full of stuff, like one giant garage sale. There's a Ping-Pong table. Dad used to talk about how he and his brother used to play all the time, but I didn't think there would be an actual table down here. There is a box of miniature records in a little square box with avocado green stripes. The Monkees. Fleetwood Mac. Kiss. Kiss? Dad liked *Kiss*? There are boxes of books—yearbooks, college annuals, cookbooks. Wardrobe boxes full of clothes. Boxes of dishes. Dad's whole childhood, pretty much, pushed against the perimeter of the building.

And then I realize I am not alone.

Uh-oh.

There it is lurking in the shadows, the overstuffed leather chair that used to be in our house. It's a huge reclining thing that Coffee chewed a chunk out of when she was a puppy. Mom and Dad had it repaired, and I guess Dad, in a fit of righteous entitlement, shoved it into the back of the delivery van and brought it here. To languish in his mother's basement. That'll show 'er.

Seeing it takes my breath away.

It doesn't belong here. It's ours. From before. When Coffee was a puppy. When we were a happy family, living our ho-hum nondramatic lives. Ours. Us. Yours. Mine. What's the difference? I run upstairs to escape the basement, swampy with my dad, to wait for the stupid clothes to finish the cycle. I am totally sick to my stomach.

Upstairs it's better. It's sunny. Clean. There is life up here. A television, a telephone, and a refrigerator full of delights. My nausea passes, leaving hunger in its wake. No time like the present to make my first Bell Jar recipe: an "avocado pear" with a hot soup of French dressing and grape jelly melted together and poured into the little bowl the pit makes. I know. But still. Avocados were Esther Greenwood's favorite "fruit." Who thinks of avocados as fruit? The same people who think of tomatoes and zucchini as fruit. It's like thinking of bacon as cake.

I think the avocado was a big deal in the 1950s. Like, a new thing that was getting imported from Mexico and Cuba or something. There were a lot of avocado green items in the fifties—dishes, Oldsmobiles, suits, dresses, etc. In The Bell Jar, after Esther has her freakout, and throws all her clothes out a high-rise window, she fills her suitcase with two dozen avocados that were a gift from her slutty friend—yes, that Doreen. And she carries this heavy suitcase around with two stripes of BLOOD on her cheek from a fight she was in with a woman-hater the night before. Who IS this Esther Greenwood? She is AMAZING.

Sometimes I just like the way Sylvia uses words. I don't mind that sometimes I have no idea what the hell she is getting at. This did not stop me from scribbling the most shocking and heartbreaking poems from <u>Ariel</u> on my tights with black Sharpie marker and wearing them to school. Which got me a dress code violation detention, and freaked Matt out so much that he started walking me to my locker between classes so I didn't get picked on by upperclassmen or do anything "crazy."

There's no actual recipe in the book, so I am winging it. I am, unlike Esther, a decent cook. It's in the genes, I think. Both my parents can whip up an amazing dinner for six from a box of pasta, a head of garlic, and a bottle of wine. So I have no qualms about my own skills. I slice an avocado in two, circling the knife around the bumpy skin and twisting the sides apart. I squirt some French dressing and a spoonful of grape jelly into a sauce pan and turn on the heat, stirring with a fork, heating it up until it is all bubbly and a dark maroon color. I find a pink plate with gray starbursts on it from Gram's Smithsonian-worthy collection and place my little avocado pear in the center and then slowly fill the little cup with the hot syrup. I raise my fork in a kind of toast to Ms. Plath and took a bite. Here are my findings:

Sofa.

King.

Delectable.

AVOCADO PEARS

On Sundays in August
You stick to the glass
Of my eye,
A stubborn raindrop.
In the center a void for me to fill
With salty sighs,
As translucent and blood-tinged as
    pomegranate seeds,
Each as soft and crunchy as hindsight.
My trajectory is undefined.

Although I did not have the forethought to pack my iPod, I brought my broken cell and charger. I found them last night in the bottom of my bag like giant (dead) cockroaches and, for the hell of it, plugged the phone in before bed.

Technology is weird. On the one hand it's really amazing. You can call, you can text, you can order boots online with your mom's credit card and they show up at your front door the next day as if you made a birthday wish and it came true. You can look up information instantly. How to tune a ukulele? How do you talk to your father after he cheated on your mom? What are the chances of a premature baby surviving after being in the NICU for two weeks? That kind of thing.

But then, technology is stupid, because it takes up a lot of time and can totally isolate you. I don't really need to tune a ukulele. I could have written an award-winning ten-volume series on the impact of Sylvia Plath on modern fiction in the hours I have frittered away becoming a fan of ridiculous pages on Facebook.

Technology's supposed to be all about connection. Right? Connection, speed, and connection speed. I mean, Matt and I text all the time, but what are we saying? Nothing, really. I mean, really? Not much. Once, Nic texted me to invite me to the grand opening of some vintage boutique on the North Side, and I texted her this: "K." I was late meeting Matt and was in kind of a hurry, which is what texting is for anyway. Because I didn't text "OK! XXOO!!" she thought I didn't really want to be there, when the truth was, I couldn't wait to join her. So, believe me, I have found out the hard way that emoticons and over-the-top cheerfulness in texts are socially necessary or people will think you're pissed off at them.

And don't even get me started on all the lead and chemicals and plastic and sweatshops and brain damage from it all. For all I know, my aunt's excessive cell phone use and Aurora's early arrival are totally related. The sonar from deep-sea oil rigs confuses dolphins so they get lost in the middle of the ocean. When I watch cable, I tune in to a minute of one show, switch over to another for a minute, a commercial comes, and I switch to a third. I toggle back and forth from one program to the other—essentially missing everything in between worth watching. Is this rewiring my brain? Probably. At least I read. Reading is perhaps the most

still, concentrated, thoughtful thing I do. Eating? Talking?
Kissing? Thinking? All low-tech activities that are cool.

Dear Technology,
    I think you are great, but I don't really think
this relationship is working.
    It's not me, it's you.
    Good luck in the future!
Best wishes,
Humanity

But then there're pacemakers, wireless ambulance tracking, laser beams, synthetic skin, and other advances that
might one day save us and our environmentally degraded
earth. All I know is, I have been without decent cable, cell
phone, and Internet access for more than two weeks and I
am still alive. I mean, Gram has lived practically her whole
life without computers, Internet, GPS, and ATMs. Like a
pioneer. Eating hardtack and hand-churned butter, getting
up to change TV channels. I'm surprised she can operate a
microwave. She looks things up—are you ready?—in a variety of bound paper resources known as a "phone book," a
"dictionary," and a "cookbook." How quaint.

Technology is supposed to be controlled by humans, and
then, just like in *The Terminator*, it comes to life and tries to
kill you. Imagine my heart attack when my phone—cracked

battery cover, missing # key, and all—vibrated back to life at three in the morning. Even though I wasn't even half awake, like a robot zombie I grabbed it and checked my messages, voice and text. All I could think was *Matt, Matt, Matt* and how much I missed him and wanted to hear from him. Anything to let me know that he can't live without me and that everything is A+ with us, and all couples have bumps in their roads and we are just as in love as ever. This is what his messages said:

MESSAGE 1: U@Keek? RU stil >8-< @ me?

MESSAGE 2: w'r @ d lake house 911 OK? If u wn2

MESSAGE 3: S yr hair stil pink?

MESSAGE 4: Do U H8 me?

MESSAGE 5: Whatev duznt m@r Nyway

How romantic. I have written reams of poetry about him, and a ream is five hundred freaking pages.

His happily married parents have a house up in Michigan they escape to every summer. I've only heard about it. I've never been. I used to think that if I were going to sleep with Matt, perhaps the lake house, or at least the beach, would be a great place for both our first times together, but I guess I missed my golden opportunity by getting the goddamned chicken pox.

"Whatever"? "Doesn't matter anyway"? He didn't hear from me in fourteen whole days and he assumed the worst? And the worst isn't chicken pox and the NICU, etc.? The worst is me ignoring him? Where is the empathy? Where is the worry? RU OK, my darling Keek? Will you ever 4give me? How I miss U!

Jock asshole.

So I texted him this:

> Ive d chikin pox
> 4 real
> V sick @ Gram's
> ParNts stil breakN ^
> MayB we shd 2

Short and sweet. When I first typed it, I thought I didn't really mean it, about breaking up, but now I know I totally did.

Breaking up. It sounds so juvenile, but believe me, I need a break from him and his mouth and his charm and his utter disregard for my well-being as he plays checkers in the lodge, aloe vera on his sunburnt nose. And what is up with him giving up on me so easily? One freaking fight, lovers' quarrel, dustup, and he's all, "Whoa, dude. Not worth the trouble. I didn't sign up for this." If anything, he should be sending me bushels of Billie Holiday hair gardenias and spiky-tongued birds of paradise, red roses, and purple starfish mum bouquets. He should be making it up to me on a daily basis for the relationship-long deception he pulled with me.

Trouble? I'll give you trouble, jackass.

All the tension, the sharing, the staring at each other's bodies in the light and in the dark, the kissing, the L, the wine, the poetry. I'm thinking about it now, and I wasn't going to type about it because it is too embarrassing and demoralizing. It is too textbook. It fits too well into my Esther Greenwoodian summer so that it seems totally contrived and ridiculous. I have been tying my brain in complicated sailor knots trying to make sense of it while simultaneously striving to avoid thinking about it.

There is not much going on in my life right now that does not infuriate me. I'm angry at, well, the parents. Amanda. Duh. Fate or whatever would make my cousin escape the womb before she was quite ready. My body for getting the stupid chicken pox. Myself, just because I'm always making regrettable decisions and messing up and misinterpreting things. But really, right this minute? As I pound out each letter in perfect two-hundred-word-a-minute typing? I am sofa king furious at—Matt.

Matt the Ratt. Oh, Sylvia would love that. That's a fact. We were in the freezer right before I got sick. Okay? For all I know that freezer is cursed. Maybe some greedy mob contractor poured the concrete for its foundation directly over an ancient Native American grave. Maybe *that* is why it is the site of such infamy, pain, betrayal, and heartbreak.

Since the whole Amanda-Dad tryst, I have pretty much avoided the freezer. But Matt swung by, all casual. I was in the back, taking pizza delivery orders, and he showed up, freshly showered after wrestling practice, smelling like Active Ice or Alpine Rain or whatever that deodorant he wears is called.

He was acting all nice. Real in-love-like. He had brought me a bunch of lilacs from his mom's garden tied up with some kitchen twine that he thrust at me like a third grader on Mother's Day. They smelled amazing. We took turns plucking the blossoms from the bunch and sucking the honey from the tiny stems.

The Active Ice, the lilacs, the honey, the soothing sound of water churning in the dishwasher—it was all really beautiful, and I actually thought, like a total adolescent idiot, how *lucky* I was to have such a great guy as my first real boyfriend. How of all the girls in the entire school, I was the only one he wanted to be with. Ha.

So we kissed a little and it was getting really hot in the back, and Matt said—*his idea*—"Let's cool off in the freezer, Keek." And for a second it was as if he'd asked me if I wanted to crawl into a coffin with a dead body and take a nap. But I got over that once he took my hand and our palms touched. Then we were standing in the center of the freezer. Swooping billows of condensation whirled around us like we were death metal rock stars. Once the steam cleared, it was as bright as an operating theater in there. Fluorescent light shone on giant jars of giardiniera and ten-pound bags of frozen French fries. I was tired and, unbeknownst to me, prepoxian. I slumped my weary body down and sat on a drum of rainbow Italian ice.

"Hey, you," he said.

I felt hyperalert, exhausted, and quivery and hot all over. "Delirious" is pushing it, but I was not myself. Being cool felt good, and my bottom lip chattered all on its own every now and again as Matt sat next to me on a pallet of tomato sauce cans and began to kiss my ear, his hand on my bouncing knee. I stopped him, sweetly. I'm nothing if not a loving sweet-as-sugar effing lollipop of a girl.

"Um, Matt."

"Um, yeah, Keek?" And he was being so cute and cuddly and koala bear-y, but I felt compelled to ask, as it was something I hadn't really asked before. Like a total SEXUAL AMATEUR.

"So, you've never, like, been with other girls before, right?" Matt is so good at all this making-out business that, what did I really think? That he'd gotten this good practicing on pillows?

"?" No words. Just a weird puzzled-liar-caught-in-the-headlights sort of moment. If we hadn't been in a freezer, Matt would have started to sweat. He wasn't looking at me but at some far-off place in the distance. Maybe looking for the cue cards with the right thing to say to me. Keek, the girl he cooked curries with and showed his spider to, and whose nipples had been in his mouth. I was regretting asking him with everything in my being, but once I started, I needed to know the answer.

"I mean, like"—and I couldn't believe he was making me say all the words out loud—"you're a virgin, same as me. Right?"

Still, silence. Crickets. I asked again, in case his jockian brain didn't understand the question. "Matt, you haven't had sex with anyone before? Have you?" I phrased it very carefully, in a high squeaky about-to-freak-out Minnie-Mouse-on-meth voice so all he had to say was no.

"Oh, hey, no way, Keek. I love you. I have been waiting my whole life up till now so you would be the first person I would ever do these things with. You are amazing and this is so special, I can't believe how lucky I am that we get to be each other's firsts." This was what he was supposed to say. But didn't. This is, actually, what he said. Ver. Ba. Tim.

"Well, er, um." And then, "Umm. Hmmm. Um, just, um—a few times. With this girl in Decatur. Um, and another girl in, um. La Grange." And just when I thought it couldn't get any worse, he said, "It was wrestling-meet craziness. Way, way before I even met you." And then. He looked at me like a drowning dog and almost started to cry. "I swear."

Decatur.

Wrestling.

Meet.

LaGrange.

Few.

Craziness.

I felt like Esther at that New York party, like I was filled with tears that were threatening to spill out and drown me if I dared let them escape—and I was really about to lose it, thinking about these girls. There is a term for these girls, and it is "ring rats." Which I am so not. They are mean. A little dumb. Wear blue eyeliner in all seriousness.

I started shivering and felt the color drain from my face and the floor disintegrate under my feet. And Matt was talking but I couldn't hear anything but this droning like a hundred bees swarming between my ears. I could hardly keep myself upright, like someone had just punched me and I couldn't breathe. And I was cold. Colder than I have ever been—and I live in Chicago.

And Matt turned toward me, his arms open to catch me or trap me or hug me, and as I stood to escape him, I pulled my cell out of the pocket of my jeans and threw it at Matt's face.

Mature, I know, but I was not the sophisticated picture of precocious wisdom and élan I usually am. My cell missed him and hit the wall and broke, and the # key chipped off, etc.

And then I calmed down—but not much. He talked a little. He said things that made me feel less unhinged, things like:

"I love you."

So?

"It's different with us."

And?

"I'll do whatever you want to do."

Because?

"I never said that I'd never done it. You just assumed I never did, and it was easier to not make a big deal out of it. It's *not* a big deal, so why are you freaking out?"

Am I?

"Anything that happened before has nothing to do with you. It's like eighth grade compared to sophomore year."

Is it?

"Please don't hate me for something I can't undo."

I'm going to puke.

"You don't look so good, Keek. Let's get out of the freezer."

Although all those things made me feel slightly better, I couldn't respond to him. My eyes blurred as I imagined my father and Amanda cavorting in the freezer, kissing and tumbling in their underwear against the very same boxes of frozen sausages and cola syrup I was bashing into on my way out the door. My mouth was as dry as paper. Maybe I was freaking out for a lot of reasons. Nothing was as it seemed. I couldn't count on anyone to be what they said they were—loyal, faithful, upstanding, attentive, Mom, Dad, best friend, virgin. I knew I should have manned-up, like Esther. She discovered way earlier than me that if you never wanted to be disappointed, you had to expect nothing from everybody. I started walking, one foot in front of the other, up to Matt and kissed him on the cheek like a brother. I slid the wilted and half-eaten lilacs in their floppy twine off the order counter into the trash, and walked all the way home, where I collapsed in a sweaty virginal heap on top of my bedspread.

Mom away.

NICU.

Chicken pox.

Gram's.

Resurrected cell phone.

Michigan.

Furious texting.

Broken up.

Absence does *not* make the heart grow fonder, apparently. And then he's going to get my letter when he gets back and be all heartbroken over me. I don't think he will ever be able to make this up to me, not in the way he thinks, anyway. He just doesn't get me. At all. And he never will. Is my hair still pink? What the hell kind of question is that? Is your pubic hair still straight? I don't know why I'm still so angry at him, but I am so furious, I want to throw stuff around my grandma's bedroom to see if it will bounce off the paneled walls and do some real damage. Heave this goddamn typewriter out the window so it lands on something beautiful and smashes it into a heap of letters and broken shit. Ram my head into the dresser mirror so it makes a giant spiderweb of cracks. Shatter the bottle of Muguet Des Bois all over the sheets. I want to light myself on fire.

Fuck.

I feel like an important part of who I am has evaporated into thin air. Weren't we crazy in love just a minute ago? Weren't we the happiest we could ever be when we were together, laughing? The safest place I knew was in your arms, you liar. This hurts. Everything hurts. My life is one stab and twist in the heart after the other.

God.

I love him sofa king much.

DATE: August 2
MOOD: Esther Greenwoodian
BODY TEMP: 100

People think The Bell Jar is all about suicide and that it is all depressing and melodramatic and what have you. They have obviously never read it. It is, in reality, very funny. Esther is a real badass and is just sick of all the ridiculousness in the world. The fashion industry. Boys. Men. Sex. The suburbs. Dieting. Academic expectations. Poetry. Hypocrisy. The same exact things that are under my skin of late.

It does, admittedly, cover some depressing territory. There are bad doctors, shock treatments, and, yes, suicide and utter despair over the state of being a woman in the world. But what I love so much about this freaking novel is that it is always the perfect book for my current mood, whatever that may be.

I mean, yes, in *real* life, the actual Sylvia Plath offed herself when she was thirty, which I used to think was old, but don't anymore because Amanda is only seven years younger.

BUT. In the semiautobiographical *novel* Esther Greenwood totally lives on and on and writes and goes off to some fancy college. She wins. And she is funny the whole time. Maybe not, like, hardee-har-har funny but knowing and cynical and able to remember how the very act of being alive puts you in situations that are ridiculous. She is able to see through all the stupid crap, especially when she is as low as you can get.

What I really can't believe about <u>The Bell Jar</u> is how nothing is really that different now. Like when people (my parents) ask what I'm going to study in college and I say, "English." They say, "Oh. So you want to be a teacher?" And I want to cover my eyes and mouth with duct tape and pretend to be *dead* and done with it.

No, you simpletons. I want to travel and write and live in a big city, and do cool things with my *brain*. This is not to disparage the fine and noble art of educating in any way. My English teachers have made me who I am today and I love them all with a passion that surprises me. I just don't want to *be* one. It's like Esther. She wants to be a serious poet. I'm talking a Nobel Prize–winning, fourth-graders memorizing you in circle time, getting your poems plastered all over the El in CTA's Poetry in Motion program kind of poet. And most people find that—charming. Like, Matt probably finds my lack of sexual experience "charming." Adorable. Cute as a fucking button. Esther/Sylvia was as serious as a nuclear bomb.

And the whole thing with her and Buddy and his Cape

Cod waitress is the same as me and Matt, kinda. I'd have thought that in the 1950s it would have been so different in that regard. That Esther even talks about sex in The Bell Jar is counterintuitive to all my assumptions about the 1950s. I'm thinking debutante balls, and *Father Knows Best*, and women wearing pearls and hats to church on Sunday, and pot roast for dinner, and little girls wearing saddle shoes and boys wearing coonskin caps. Cars with fins. I have never (I mean, before The Bell Jar) thought of the 1950s as a time when girls with blood on their cheeks could run around with suitcases full of avocados. Girls could get drunk with sex-crazed cowboys. Girls could try to kill themselves because it's all sofa king depressing.

And really, for Esther to decide that her boyfriend is lower than dirt because he is a hypocrite who is not the virgin she thought he was the whole time they were going together, which ruins him for her forever, is pretty punk rock. She is, as much as she can be in those up-tight and conservative times, true to herself and to her own desires. Which is cool in any era. And precisely what I need to be reading about right now, what with Matt's deception and all.

Despite his usually magnificent and gentlemanly behavior, Matt was more of a con artist than I realized. When you are so in love with a person, you tend to overlook their faults. You register the slights, the odd behaviors, the tiny betrayals, and collect them in a little velvet bag you wear on your hip. I have collected hurts with my father. My darling mother. Best-Friend-of-the-Year-Award-Winning Amanda. And I have, until recently, been able to look past them all. As long as these people were not directly hurting me, my screwed-up logic went, they could do what they liked.

But then when dad and Amanda "hooked up"—a phrase that is so indistinct and deceptively casual, I find it insulting—I started to remember all the crappy things she said and did since we first started hanging out. And I felt stupid that I didn't see it coming. Amanda really had me fooled. She sweet-talked me through her tales of experience with her spectacular sense of humor. I ignored my true self, which was trying to warn me. It was like the smoke detector in my soul was filled with dead batteries. Maybe if I had kept Nic around, she could have warned me. Maybe if I had done a lot of things, then a lot of other things would have never happened at all. Live and learn.

So when Matt pulled his big non-virginity reveal in the freezer, it added to the pile of everything else going wrong in my life, and his betrayal was more than I could bear. The oh-by-the-way-I'm-not-a-virgin thing should have broken us up then and there, but I didn't have the strength. I had the chicken pox.

Breaking up only a couple weeks later via text is no easier. It is horrible. But maybe I'm a little different now. I'm turning into a Teflon-coated version of the old Keek. It's not like Matt has always been a paragon of steadfast loyalty and love. He has epically let me down before, and I let it slide.

Crap. Dinner. Gram's calling me from the kitchen.

This will have to be a story for another day.

Right. There was a piercing, okay? We were out—me, Matt, and Earl the Squirrel. We took the Metra train downtown and then the El to Clark and Belmont and tried to fit in with all the other people hanging around the tattoo shop who seemed much older, like they were in college.

I wasn't myself then. I was going through every motion more slowly, as if I had wet sand in my veins—brushing my teeth, writing papers for English, eating fries at the D&D. It was like I was standing still as the world whirled past me, blurry, while I stared into space.

And let me tell you, this shop was nothing if not a hullabaloo. We didn't plan it, really. Earlier that night we had just been hanging out. We drank coffee at Dunkin' Donuts and then went to that store the Alley and poked around, bought some stupid stickers for our nonexistent skateboards and book bags. Earl the Squirrel tried on some rings with glass eyes in them and put his fist in my face and said, "Here's lookin' at you, kid," which was actually kinda funny.

The store was enormous with high ceilings and just covered with your typical angsty subversive crap—biker wallets, skull and crossbones belt buckles, the aforementioned Manic Panic hair dye, outrageous hoodies with pinup girls on them. You know the stuff I'm talking about. In a word, amazing. Then we were looking at the fancy body jewelry in the case, and I said, "Matt, let's get our tongues pierced."

What? Did I say that? What the hell was I thinking? First of all—I mean, ouch. It looks really cool on others, but on me? I was just feeling so "Up yours, World" that right then I thought putting a hole and metal barbell in my tongue made all kinds of sense. I had done research on it ages before, and it turns out that there is a place on your tongue that has no feeling in it. It's like a dead space between the two halves of muscle. When they pierce, this is where they are putting the hole. I know. Cool or what?

And then it became this big thing. Earl the Squirrel started chanting, "Pierce! Me! Pierce! Me! Pierce! Me!" and we were all on fire to do it, or at least to have one of us do it.

When we got to the tattoo shop, it was obvious—they thought we were children. My face was hot with embarrassment at Earl the Squirrel's braces and wrestling sweatshirt, and our wrinkle-free skins. Matt, who is not a big guy, still seemed like the most mature because he looked at me and then waltzed right up to the counter and said to this woman with bright red hair in a 1940s hairdo and *horns implanted in her forehead* and arms like colored Sunday comics, "Good evening. I'd like to get my tongue pierced, please." I don't know if he was showing off for me—his sad girlfriend he was trying to bed—or his wrestling teammate and local spaz about town, but it didn't matter. Are you seeing why I was so into him?

For a demon girl she was supernice and cheerful. "Hi, guys. Are you eighteen?" I wanted to just melt like the Wicked Witch of the West into a puddle on the floor because, duh, we were not eighteen. "Sorry, guys, but in the state of Illinois you need to be eighteen to get pierced without your parents' permission."

We were so lame. We huddled in a corner to discuss. I wanted to run all the way to Union Station and get the first train back to the suburbs and my miserable house with my depressed parents, but I also wanted someone to get something pierced. The idea of metal sliding through skin seemed so elegant and beautiful. It seemed like the best way to feel better about things, another outward statement about how screwed-up things felt on the inside.

Matt understood, because he took my hand. He said, "I'm doing this, okay? For you, Keek."

And I said, "For me?" And then he kissed me, hard, in front of everyone, his smooth unpierced tongue giving me a quick lick on its way out, an electric zing running all the way down to my underwear.

Matt told the tattooed demon girl, "I'll be eighteen in, like, eight months." He was exaggerating (he just turned seventeen this May, and the piercing was last November), but still. "Then I'll have to register at the post office so if they need to draft me, I can go off and kill people. If they don't kill me first." And then he said this: "Is. That. Eighteen. Enough?" Hot or what?

She looked at me and Earl the Squirrel like we were pathetic orphans. Then she said to Matt, "I can do your eyebrow, fast and in the back. Your girlfriend can come with, but, dude, that friend of yours has to wait up front."

Before I go on, let me just say that Chicago at night is especially beautiful. I've never been to New York but feel as if I have because of Esther Greenwood's internship in The Bell Jar, and it seems pretty and all, but I know for a fact how amazing Chicago is. Illinois is flat. As a pancake, as a plate. When we went to the Sears Tower (or the Willis Tower, though no true Chicagoan would be caught dead calling it that) in grade school and looked down at the city, I could see far and wide—streets and highways and shiny glass buildings and then suburbs and farther out grass and what looked like farms. The lake on the other side, as wide and deep as the ocean with water so fresh and blue it seemed to go out and out and out forever.

At night Chicago is a clear and glittering city with a great yawn of blackness where the lake is. It is the City, and anything is possible. It is not your parents' house. It is not their basement. It lies before you, offering itself like a black sequined dress on a bed before a school dance. All you have to do is go there and be you and live, because everything is yours for the taking. Out the window of the tattoo shop at Clark and Belmont, the El tracks rumbled overhead, and sushi restaurants' lanterns glowed red. Teenagers dressed in black from all over Chicagoland roamed the streets looking for love, for weed, for trouble, and the air crackled with danger and adulthood and possibilities.

So when I followed Matt and Demon Girl to the back room, I wasn't scared or even a little freaked out. I was ready. She leaned Matt back in a chair, like a barber's chair. She put on purple latex gloves. She disinfected Matt's eyebrow with an alcohol square. She took a skinny hollow needle from a wrapper like the kind string cheese comes in. Matt looked at the ceiling. She leaned over, and I'm sure he tried to see the dragons down her cleavage, but I didn't care.

Using a scissors clamp, she grabbed a part of his left eyebrow and swabbed it with numbing stuff. And one, two, three, the needle was through the thinnest part of his left eyebrow and then she expertly (she probably does this fifteen times a day) slipped a small silver hoop with a little ball on it through, swabbed more goo on with an extra long Q-tip, and forty dollars later, we were done.

Watching wasn't as cool as I thought it would be. It was like seeing someone get a boil lanced. But he did it. That part was amazing. My boyfriend pierced his eyebrow. For me. And it looked sofa king hot. And I felt powerful and invincible and taller and totally like Lady Lazarus in Sylvia's poem—on fire and ready for whatever the night would bring.

As soon as we emerged into the front room, Earl the Squirrel jumped up and said, "That shit's hot, yo. But Coach isn't gonna let you keep it." And as soon as he said it, we all knew it was true. But I felt that Matt and I had crossed a threshold that night and that we understood each other on a new deeper and fundamental level. That he understood, through the intensity of our love, what his eyebrow ring represented: us. He'd never get rid of it, for Coach Pernaki or anyone else. They would have to pry that eyebrow ring from his cold dead corpse before he'd remove it for anyone, for any reason, ever, because *that was how much he loved me.*

He didn't even wait one freaking week.

That Wednesday before practice Matt kissed me and then headed off to the locker room with his eyebrow ring intact. When he met me at the D&D after practice, he didn't even mention it. I had to be the one to say "Where is it? You're putting in back in, right? Right?" And then I said,

"RIGHT?" again like I had Tourette's syndrome. And then he said, "Come on, Keek. It was a goof. You know, for kicks. I can't keep that crap in my face. I mean, come on."

See? *This* is where I should have broken up with him. Like, "That's it. We are so done. And to think that I was contemplating doing it with you, you selfish jock bastard." But that was not how I felt. The wounds were fresh. He still had two holes on his eyebrow like a vampire bat had bitten him.

I just said, "Well. Tell Coach that Keek says, 'Hey.'" And I left my own restaurant. Which was also pretty dramatic.

It still stings, a little, that Matt gave me up so easily. "Oh? This little eyebrow ring? It's nothing. Here, I'll remove it right now and toss it over my shoulder like a piece of used Kleenex. Who cares?"

I know, I know. He is a wrestler, and a good one. An eyebrow ring is dangerous, to him and his opponents. It is against Illinois High School Association rules and regulations to have any facial piercings in competitive sports, blah, blah, blah. But I was holding on to that eyebrow ring for dear life. Its very presence on his face let the world know that we were having an impact on each other, he was making changes for me. He was putting little holes in his face to prove his love, and as long as Matt wore it, we were okay, everything was okay, everything was going to be okay.

When that was not the case.

At all.

I know, I know, I know. Matt's non-virginity should have been obvious if I had been paying any attention whatsoever. At least Matt's as hot as all get-out. I think Esther's whole problem with Buddy is not only that he is not a virgin but also that he is a mama's boy doofus. She is smart and accomplished. Her vision of the world is multifaceted—nuanced and beautiful. She is ambitious. And then he goes and tells her about some old waitress that he did it with all summer long. And I think—no, I *know* because I have been there— her whole crisis over Buddy's revelation had to do with how she now saw herself. Suddenly she was infantilized. Her sexual longings and small experiments in nakedness were suddenly quaint, or some such crap, to Buddy. The total dipwad fathead.

Matt is no dipwad. Esther wasn't jealous. She was furious. I am furious and a little jealous. Of ring rats, of all things. They are the kinds of girls who beat up other girls in bathrooms to exert authority and pecking order upon pink-haired honors English girls like me. They are a bunch of gumsnapping, slutty Doreens. Matt. Honestly. How could you?

Esther says that Buddy always acted like she was so much more experienced than him. He acted as if she were inspiring new intense feelings he had never had before because of her inherent sexiness, which, for a poet, would be, like, important. Hell, it would be important to any artistic honors English virgin. She felt duped. As do I.

Buddy also, throughout the whole <u>Bell Jar</u>, acts like a complete buffoon. He's in freaking medical school but is a total rube when it comes to real feelings and real life. Matt is not like that at all. He has guts. He likes to make me feel good and has never tricked me into doing anything I didn't want to do. I know I shouldn't be as mad as I am. It's a pride thing. He should have told me, that's all. He should have told me and just put it out there, and I could have recovered earlier instead of later—meaning now, when I'm sick and alone and in the middle of this soul-destroying summer.

I'm sofa king sick of finding out all kinds of intense personal crap by total accident.

DATE: August 4
MOOD: A Gaper's Delay on My Mom's Trajectory
BODY TEMP: 99

MOM: Hi, Keekie. Oh, my darling. How are you feeling?

ME: Hi, Mom!

MOM: I e-mailed you some pictures of Aurora. Have you seen them?

ME: No. Internet. Here. Remember? (Honestly.)

MOM: Oh, right. Well, when I get back, you'll see.

ME: When's that gonna be? Never?

MOM: No, next week, like I said. Are you being nice to Gram? I hope you're not causing any trouble for her. That lady's been through a lot, you know.

ME: Oh, I know. She's pretty cool. Mom?

MOM: Yesss?

ME: I think Matt and I broke up. I mean, it's not like you and Dad or anything, but. I dunno. It's so over. Dunzo, I think.

And then, dear reader, I started to cry.

AND THEN I SAID: Everything is so screwed-up, and I feel like crap. I just feel like absolute crap about everything.

MOM: Oh, Karina. I'm so sorry. I'm so sorry about everything. I thought I was doing the right thing. I really had no choice. Being an adult is just as shitty as being fifteen.

ME: What are you talking about?

MOM: Haven't you talked to your father?

ME: I haven't talked with Dad in, like, two and half weeks, Mom. He's always at the D&D, and then home sleeping, and then back to work.

MOM: I'll be home soon. We can talk then, Keek. I gotta go. It's peak usage time here. Love you.

ME: Mom—

MOM:

ME: Love you too.

When I have a daughter with the chicken pox and I call her long distance to say hello and she starts to weep into the receiver about her broken heart, I will remember to ask her more questions. I will be kinder and more interested in her goings-on. I will not bring up the phone company's billing methods. I will not talk about my own relationship issues.

I will be the mother.

And I ask you, how can being an adult *ever* be as shitty as being fifteen? If I were sixteen, at least I'd have a driver's license and a sweet sixteen birthday bash. I'd fit a certain marketing bracket like a glove. But I am fifteen, which is too close to thirteen and too far from eighteen to be of any real use to anyone. I'm independent and totally dependent. I'm a kid. I'm not. I'm mature for my age instead of just being my age. I'm old enough to know better but too young to do anything on my own. I feel ancient.

Online spiritual advisers say that if you ask a kid younger than five years old "Who were you before you were here?" they will tell you with all honesty, and with no shame, who they were in a past life. I read that on some website my mom had up on her Mac. I don't really know any little kids to ask, but I would love to try to find some.

Most people in school talk about how they were Marilyn Monroe or Hemingway. And I'm always, like, why the hell would Marilyn Monroe or Hemingway show up in some suburb of Chicago and be in high school? Reading makes me feel like I've lived a thousand lives in addition to my own. Characters in books really stick around for me. You know cartoon cells, the translucent sheets they draw on to make cartoons? Every time I read a book, especially one that grabs my guts, there is another translucent layer added to what makes me, me. Each layer is saturated in color and signed by the artist. I mean, yes, I think I have been on earth before, but reading books that illuminate and explore what it means to be alive sometimes makes me feel as wise and powerful as Cleopatra.

Once when I was in fifth grade (only five years ago!), I read an entire Trixie Belden mystery that I found on the sale table at the library. On Gram's porch in one afternoon, I read and read and drank an entire pitcher of iced tea until the book was finished and my bladder was the size of a volleyball. That's how I roll.

I mean, I like movies, too. All kinds. Technicolor, musicals, black-and-white, rom coms, bromances, thrillers, animated shorts, documentaries, chick flicks, dramas, foreign, sci-fi, *Chimps in Space*, whatever. Love them all. They are yet one more way to learn about living. Books and movies, they are not mere entertainment. They sustain me and help me cope with my real life.

Speaking of real life, what the holy hell is up with my mother? "Thought I was doing the right thing"? "I really had no choice"? Dad's the one who decided to ruin everything for some dirtbag in his employ. As far as I can tell, Mom didn't do anything but work her fingers to the bone and meditate, feed Coffee, and make sure the carpets got vacuumed on a regular basis. She was betrayed, and, speaking as an expert on betrayal, she should really stop beating herself up about it, or at least stop being so nice to her adulterous, lying, cheating, selfish heap of garbage soon-to-be ex-husband, aka Dad. Why are women—and I mean most women I know or see on TV—so ready to take the blame for everything and so ready to apologize for everything? My mom is always saying "Sorry" when what she means is "What? I didn't hear you," or "Excuse me," or "Please don't be mad at my decision." The only person she never says sorry to is me.

My head hurts. A glass of Sabor Latino juice, a little Tylenol, and it's good night, Chicago.

When I asked Gram what shock treatments feel like, she took a while to answer me. She didn't really want to go into detail. After our whole chicken pox blood experience, we are closer than ever, but I'm surprised she told me about it in the first place. I still expect my mom to be, like, my capital-M Mom. But my grandma is a different type of mom to me. She can be the world's oldest showgirl; she can be my best friend; she can be a life inspiration or a life warning; but whatever she is, she is connected to me in intense and unique ways. And I'm kind of into her since the bath, the heart-to-heart, and the vintage clothes bonanaza.

Despite reading my pages, she has never lied to me. And although I was totally aggravated that she invaded my privacy, at least she was extremely interested in me and my life and my writing and the goings-on in my brain, which is more than I can say about either one of my parents, or even Matt. Besides, I could have confronted her about it, but I didn't. For all I know it was all in my paranoid poxian imagination.

There's this Plath poem called "Kindness" all about, um, kindness sliding through the house with cups of tea. And so now I think of Gram as Dame Kindness without any irony and in all seriousness.

We were making teacups of raw hamburger and egg, recipe number two on my Bell Jar recipe list. I was a little grossed-out, but then Gram said in the 1950s she used to put the same raw egg and raw hamburger mixture between white bread with mayonnaise and ketchup and call it a cannibal sandwich. Which didn't make it any more appetizing, but made me determined to at least take one bite.

I was mashing raw egg (raised on vegetarian feed, with extra omega-3s) and ground beef (organic grain-fed and humanely raised and slaughtered) with a fork and got the ball rolling by asking Gram what Myrna Loy looked like. Esther says that her last and beloved therapist looked like Myrna Loy, and I assumed Ms. Loy was blond and perky/pretty like Doris Day. But no. Myrna Loy had a heart-shaped face and black hair and was, in Gram's words, "drop-dead gorgeous and as smart as a whip," which makes so much sense. Of course Esther would appreciate a witty, intelligent, and sophisticated therapist over a replacement mother. And then I took a deep breath and just asked, "So, Gram. What did shock treatments really feel like?"

Without stopping, she kept mashing her meat and egg and said that it didn't hurt. That her brain was so messed-up that the shock felt like jumping into a freezing swimming pool until she was numb. Afterward she rested in a sunny hospital room until her brain slowly warmed up enough to think rational thoughts. Gram had three treatments, was in the hospital for three months, and didn't really want to say much more.

In <u>The Bell Jar</u>, Esther describes shock treatments as a thousand times more bone-shaking and loud and violent.

"Did you try to kill yourself?" I didn't really think about it then, but now I'm wondering, what if she had said, "Oh, boy, did I! I took pills by the handful," or "I let the Saturn idle in the garage with the door shut and breathed deep while I waited to die," or worse. And then what could I have possibly said?

Luckily, she said, "No. I didn't. But I wasn't eating. I slapped a salesgirl at Marshall Field's because they didn't have a shoe in my size. I put bright red lipstick above and below my lips so I looked like Bozo the Clown. I was sadder than I had ever been in my entire life, and I couldn't bear it anymore. I just couldn't bear being alive." She placed our teacups of meat on saucers and fanned crackers around the base of the cups.

"Back then shock treatments were the knee-jerk prescription for anyone who was severely depressed. Shock therapy or pills, usually both. But I got better. Your dad was away at the University of Wisconsin, and I wanted to be myself again, for him at least. I did it, and I'm fine now, but sometimes, Karina, life can overwhelm you. The trick is to put your head down and just get on with it. I got a little weak and succumbed to the despair. I'm not proud of it. I don't talk about it. I just wanted to let you know that I've been through worse things than what's going on with your parents, and survived. You will, you know."

"Will what?" I asked. I was still mulling over the brain-on-ice thing. After her shock treatments Esther compared her brain to an ice skater doing figure eights somewhere on a giant deserted pond, and I knew my Gram was being real with me.

"Survive, Keek." And she smiled. "Eat your cannibal cup."

On a cracker, it wasn't so bad.

Funny how you think you're such a smart-ass know-it-all, and then the curtain is pulled back and what you thought is the real story was not the whole story. I feel like I have been living in the Pulitzer Prize–winning stage production of Karina's life. Starring Karina as Keek. I am just faking it until I figure what the hell to do next. I like to think I have X-ray vision and "know" people, but it turns out that I have been wrong on all counts—that is, Amanda, Dad, Matt, Gram, Mom. What goes on inside your head and heart is entirely private. At least I know who/what the hell I am. I don't reveal much to the outside world. Mostly it's all here, on these pages. I'll let it out one day, soon. When I'm ready. Right now it's easier keeping the pages locked away. Bolted up. Surrounded by laser beams like the Mona Lisa at the Louvre. Which means upside down, beneath a short stack of outdated *Prevention* magazines in my dead great-grandma's underwear drawer.

DATE: August 6
MOOD: Weary and Lava-boned
BODY TEMP: 98.6 *stadium cheering*

My pox are gone for the most part, but I'm still as tired as a malaria patient. It is probably more depression than anything else, but whatev, I need my rest. So I'm lying on the couch in the front room, waiting for sleep or the loneliness cat to pounce on me, when my pathetic limping phone vibrates to life on the floor next to the end table. And it is—Matt. The nonvirgin scoundrel.

> Hey K! Im bak frm d lake :)!

And for a minute there—maybe even five entire minutes—forget that I am mad at him, that he is my XBF, that I am ignoring his attempts at communicating. My head is swimming with love and I text him this:

> ME: QL

MATT: Hw RU? Stil got chikin pox?

ME: FeelN mch btr. Mis U.

MATT: M2

ME: I h8 my dad ryt nw. Totes dpresd

MATT: Y?

Matt knows all about Dad and Amanda. He was at the restaurant practically as much as I was. But I never told Matt all the sordid and painful emotional details. I was too embarrassed. I made it seem like I was made of tougher stuff, that this kind of ridiculous soap opera behavior had no significant impact on me. Ha. If this happened to Matt's parents, he would be furious, like the-Hulk-ripping-his-shirt-off incensed. Me? I'm always a little enraged, with a dish of dejected on the side. Would you like betrayed with that? No substitutions. And when Matt flat out asks me why I am so depressed, without my brain thinking about it, my fingers type this into my keypad.

Evry1 I care bout hs betryd me. Evry1 dz whtev the hell thy wnt and nvr thnks hw it mght affect me. Nt jst dad n Amanda but u & mom & evn Nic a lil. Whr r u?

Okay. That looks absolutely ridiculous in text. But that is it in a nutshell. Hurt, shattered, deceived, etc. My father slept with someone I knew and didn't even think about what it might do to me. I'm someone he's supposed to care about more than anything else in the world. Amanda didn't think of me at all, I'm sure, as she flung her bony self against my father all over the cold storage items. And I'm waiting for Matt's answer, because I think that it might help me feel closer to him. Or at least make me laugh. I'm waiting and waiting in the heat for what feels like an hour.

People—and by that I mean the media, weathermen, late-night comedians—go on and on about how cold Chicago is. *Brrrrr,* and blizzards and digging cars out of snowbanks and "Oh, the hardy Midwesterner can handle all weather." No one talks about how Chicago gets so hot you can fry eggs on car hoods and how it goes from winter to summer in sixty seconds flat. No spring to speak of. I don't remember spring this year. Maybe it happened and I was too caught up in my own hullabaloo to notice. And now that it is August and I'm not shivering with a fever, it is unbelievably hot. Sweat drips down my back and over whatever pox scabs remain, making me fidget as I sit there waiting for Matt to text something—anything. And then this:

MATT: it tAkz 2 2 tango

ME: ?

MATT: @(*o*)@

What is up with boys? And no acknowledgment that I broke up with him. Maybe the text was too nuanced for his jockian brain. Or maybe he isn't going to let me break up with him by text. Maybe he loves me so much that he thinks if he ignores it, it will go away. Whatever confusion has kept us alive and whole is fine by me. Besides, I know the koala bear is our code for "I love you." And then I see Matt's beaten-down old, black VW Golf (Wolfsburg edition) pull up in front of Gram's house, and I proceed to watch him try to parallel park for fifteen minutes.

He is here! And I think *I am excited! But not really*. I'm going to let our bodies do the talking. See what happens. See if my body has forgiven him. Bodies don't lie. Right?

DATE: August 7
MOOD: There Are No Words

It wasn't Matt's idea, but he inspired the whole thing. God, he is sofa king beautiful. This whole time, typing about him and every other little thing on this IBM typewriter, I forgot how real-life good he feels and tastes and forgot how much I can't wait to see him again every time we leave each other. But I know we're not getting married or anything. He doesn't really read enough. Oh, he reads. But not enough, not for fun. He's really all about his body. We're going to different colleges for sure, so what's the point?

To be fair, when push came to shove, he was honest with me, at least. About the virginity, I mean. Unlike both of my parents, he can look me in the eye and tell me things I should know just because I deserve to know. Now I think that we were meant to be together. During this time in both our lives. I know it sounds dramatic, but maybe when I'm, like, thirty or whatever I will look back wistfully at my awesome high school boyfriend. It will probably all end terribly and in tears, and I might find out (but most likely not) that besides the sexual adventuring with the ring rat brigade, he totally made out with that Keds-wearing freshman. But today, right now, I'm glad he's around.

When he said, "It takes two to tango," he was just trying to be funny. But as we sat in his car with the air on, I was, like, *yeah, two to tango*. As he leaned the seats back as far as they could go and ran his warm hand up from my waist to my chest with his mouth on mine, I thought, *What would make me give up all this kind of happiness with Matt?* And I remembered that when I was alone and totally unhappy—just days ago—I had, in all seriousness and with much hatred in my heart, *broken up with him*. That was when I knew there was way more to this divorce than some stupid sexcapade between Dad and Amanda, and if my so-called parents didn't have the guts or time to talk with me about it, I had to take matters into my own hands. I mean, and I don't say this lightly, WTF?

Sometimes you need to know things. Especially things that directly impact your life and emotional well-being. And let me say right now, for the record, if I were on trial in Judge Judy Sheindlin's courtroom, this would be my only defense for my actions.

Unlike Gram, my parents' mouths have been shut as tight as clams about anything important that has anything to do with anything I care about. And I have had it. Gram can talk about one of the most degrading and upsetting experiences of her life while eating raw meat, but my dumb-ass parents can't even sit me down over coffee to explain what has happened to our family and their marriage. Which, at this point, is the same thing.

I had to look for answers, and now I sorta wish I hadn't, because things are sofa king messed up. All I am capable of doing right now is typing, and using my involuntary muscles to swallow and blink.

So, after making out with Mutant Frogboy and trying to hide my hormonal upheaval from Gram, I went down to the basement on a long-overdue fact-finding mission. Dame Kindness was upstairs. Every once in while I heard her footsteps creak from the front room to the back porch, or from the dining room to the kitchen. I told her it was cooler in the basement. I brought down a glass of lemonade and my battered copy of <u>The Bell Jar</u> to complete the ruse. I had no intention of drinking or reading anything in the basement. Instead I stood in front of the door to the Lair. I waited for Gram's feet to wander to the front room, the place farthest away from where I was below.

The door to the Lair was cheap, covered in gray laminate. The knob was gold with a hole in the center that you couldn't peek through, but could be used to pick open the lock if you had to. I didn't have to because it was open.

My dad was where he always was since he moved here—

out. Working. Working. Working some more. Hi ho, hi ho, it's off to work I go. Working. I even said something to him the other day. As he walked out the door, I said, "See ya never." I thought he would think that I was saying "See you later," but he was actually listening to me, and he turned in the doorway and said, "I know, Keek. I'll come back early tonight. Maybe we can go for ice cream."

At first I was, like, *Yippee, ice cream!* But then I remembered that I could never be purely happy again, that I'm not six, I'm fifteen, and ice cream wasn't going to make me feel one iota better. And I said, "Whatever." And meant it.

I thought of this as I turned the knob and pushed. Doors. Walking through them, opening them, shutting them. They are part of everyone's day-to-day life, but as I passed from basement to Lair, I felt in my bones that I was transgressing something important like trust, privacy, personal rights. I was crossing the threshold into my dad's shame because I could and because I needed to. So there I was, smack-dab in the center of his room, the sanctuary, the tomb. His capital-L Lair.

There was a prefab homework desk beneath the window, which was covered with papers scattered like leaves on a curb. There was a dresser with grooming things on it. There was an unmade bed, big enough for only one person. A built-in bookcase held some tax books and a framed picture of me when I was eight—braids, missing teeth, etc.

The windows looked out onto the backyard, the pavement, and the grass beyond. It was a foxhole. It was a child's room. It smelled like a greasy man and/or a gerbil lived there. I suddenly imagined my dad as a kid on the debate team sitting in the school cafeteria, eating fries. I know from old pictures that he was a skinny teenager, and I could see him, sitting here at his desk finishing a geometry assignment before slipping some cash into his jeans' pocket and meeting friends for Cokes or to buy Kiss records.

On the dresser, one hairbrush. Tortoiseshell with black plastic bristles and a broken handle. Who else would brush their hair with such a ridiculous implement but my father? It used to be my mom's. She brushed her hair with it, my hair with it, and even today I'm sure if some voodoo priestess wanted to place curses on us, she could get samples from this very brush. The point being, it was an artifact from his old life. Like the leather recliner in the sitting area and the picture of me in the bookcase, the brush was one more thing that Dad needed in order to get through his day-to-day life in this house without his wife and, I suppose, daughter. Creepy. Or not so creepy. Just sad. Sofa king sad that I just sat in the desk chair. Numb. You can only go so long saying to yourself, "This can't be happening, this can't be happening," before you just have to stop saying it, hold still, and let it sink in.

Sunlight angled through the basement windows onto

the desk, and now that I'm typing this, it was like God or the director of a telenovela beamed a spotlight right on the freaking Holy Grail. It was like angels should have been singing opera at the discovery. At first I thought they were just papers. Adult nonsense, like tax stuff or Dine & Dash invoices for vent cleaning. But then I looked closely, like *CSI*-forensics closely, and they weren't your ordinary flotsam and jetsam of business-owning waste-paper. They were letters. Bank statements. Copies of receipts. All from the last few months. Words and columns, letters and numbers, all tic-tac-toeing across the papers like code.

My heart was beating sofa king fast. I knew it was try-ing to tell me that I should turn back, that this wasn't fair or right, but when passing an accident on the Eisenhower Expressway, I couldn't look away. I sat in the desk chair and took deep breaths while I tried to really see things for what they were. But each time I looked at one piece of evidence, I had to look at something else. To see if anything hidden away down here would tell me what I needed to know about my parents, about me, about what was going to happen to all of us.

When my parents first started counseling, Mom stopped mentioning Amanda in conversation, but I didn't think much of it. The phone would ring at weird times and Mom would pick up the phone and say something cryptic like,

"Don't" or "He's not here," when he so was right there, in the repaired leather recliner, holding his head in his hands. And sweating.

Something was rotten in Denmark, right? But I couldn't tell where the smell was coming from. Dear reader, I was oblivious. I also wasn't seeing much of Amanda then. School was busy and our schedules were different, and again, it didn't mean anything in particular to me.

I'll never forget the night I found out. After weeks of therapy my parents seemed to be enjoying a night of renewed domestic bliss. For real. I remember how peaceful and secure I felt in the living room, listening to my parents being nice to each other for a change. Mom and Dad, probably inspired by their therapist, decided to make a big pot of red sauce from scratch and had been bumping into each other in the kitchen like drunk bumblebees all afternoon. They seemed to be having the time of their lives, and the house smelled amazing. I thought however much they were paying this amazingly gifted marriage counselor was not enough.

They opened a second bottle of wine. I was in the living room, living. I could see them through the kitchen doorway and hear their teasing and cajoling escalate into something sharper, louder. I got up to get a Coke from the fridge. Trying, I guess, to keep them from fighting. It was like I was trying to prevent two betta fish cheerfully circling each other from realizing they were mortal enemies.

And then I heard it—from Mom. She threw a wooden spoon heavy with sauce at the wall and screamed: "At least I didn't screw the WAITSTAFF."

The what staff?

?

The only two waitstaff were me and—

?

So.

?

It must have been . . .

?

—

Oh.

God.

I was right there when she said it. I looked at my Dad, who was at once repugnant and pathetic, then at the splash of red on the wall where the spoon had hit. It looked like a bullet had gone through his forehead and splattered his brains all over the place. And my mom was standing there, the opposite of Zen, with both hands clamped over her mouth like a speak-no-evil monkey.

I grabbed my iPod and left. Went walking. Where? Around the blocks of our idyllic suburban neighborhood, but I don't remember a thing of it. Only that it was the colorless, silent landscape of the shocked.

It was suddenly as if I had never had a father. I felt this

void in my head and heart where my dad usually inhabited. So total was my pain, it was like he had never existed. It was as if someone had torn my plug out of the wall. Everything was deadened and more silent than silent, because there was no energy pulsing through anything.

Now that we are cloistered together here at Gram's house, he's slowly taking form again. I catch glimpses of him when he pops his head into my room to check on me before heading down to the Lair, or as he takes the garbage out for Gram. He is working, yes, but I know he is also avoiding me because he is humiliated by his own behavior. If I were him, I'd lie low too.

That stunning night of dismay when it all came out was the very worst I thought I could feel about the goings-on in my parents' marriage—when, ha, ha, ha. Little did I know the outrages that awaited. Like the evidence before me: the D&D's bank statements.

The bank records were pretty straightforward. At first glance, they seemed as innocent and meaningless as a grocery receipt. And yet a floundering Algebra II student could interpret them with the greatest of ease.

In layman's terms, the restaurant was screwed.

There was no money in the Dine & Dash, Inc., account.

$0.00.

Then a letter from the bank saying, "Thank you for banking with us. If there is anything we can do for you in future, do not hesitate blah, blah, blah." And then bills, big ones for D&D insurance, workers' compensation premiums, meat delivery, etc. So of course I'm convinced that skanky and manipulative Amanda took advantage of my family, broke my mother's heart, *and* swindled all this money out of my poor overworked, under-loved, sex-starved Dad, when I see my *mother's* ridiculously flamboyant signature beneath the reams of legalese.

There was a letter underneath all these papers, hand-written, on stationery from Hallmark or something. I'm just going to attach it here as evidence. Besides, retyping it would re-break my heart. Let me warn you: It is not very Zen. My mother has a trajectory, all right. She can go straight to hell.

Dear Kevin,

I don't expect you to understand, but I need to have a fulfilling life. Although I care for you, you know as well as I do that something has changed.

But I need financing. I've closed the D+D account and am going to use the cash to help me rebuild my life. You are a better businessperson than I am and can run the restaurant without me. You'll be better off without me. I promise.

I have been very unhappy and couldn't see any other way to break free.

Please don't hate me,

Love always,

L

DATE: August 8
MOOD: As Nude as a Chicken Neck

How long did Dame Kindess watch Matt and me make out before tapping on the window? Oh, yeah, I should have typed that up yesterday, but there are so many humiliations of late that, forgive me if I forget to mention them all in chronological order.

When I say "making out" I mean *making out*. In an idling car. With the air on in the thousand-degree sun. During the day. In front of my grandmother's house. It had been more than three weeks. And more than that, when I'm with Matt, all this other monstrous crap gets put on hold. Making out with him is like entering a suspension pod in a sci-fi movie. It's like taking a nap from your life. And if anyone deserves a break, it's me.

And so Matt's got his hand up my shirt, and my underwear is totally soaked and I'm feeling like a lady baboon with all my pink parts inflamed, and then *knock, knock, knock* on the VW window. I swear I have never seen Matt move so fast, not even in the wrestling ring.

It was Gram. Smoking, a hand on her hip, acting like an extra from a Joan Crawford movie. And we were newly sweating and red in the face, and I was a slug upon whom salt had just been poured.

"Out," Gram said. I opened the door and slithered out onto the hot pavement.

She said, "Keek, telephone." And then she said, to Matt, "I'm Karina's grandma. Who the hell are you?"

And I started to say something but got this laser beam look, so off I went to get the phone.

Mom. I could hardly think straight—what with my sexed-up blood a-jangle in my nerve endings—let alone talk to Mom, but here is what I learned:

1. Aurora was out of the hospital. (Yes!)
2. Mom as coming home on Monday. (La. Dee. Freaking. Da.)
3. Then she said, "We need to talk."
4. And I didn't know then about the embezzling, but if I had, I would have said, "Fuck you."
5. Instead I said, "Okay, Mom. Call me again tomorrow," like an utter simp. But she didn't call me back. Chicken.

When I got back outside, Matt was gone. The sun was moving lower in the sky, and Gram said, "How about an early supper of broiled tomato and Spam?" (Recipe number three on my Bell Jar recipe list.)

Now, normally I hate the word "supper." It seems like a word a toddler would make up because she couldn't say the word "dinner." I also have issues with the words "knapsack" (why not backpack?) and "poncho" (you have to move your mouth too much to say it). But I didn't have the piss and vinegar needed to quibble with Gram about words when she was being so respectful about what was a very delicate situation.

As much as I do not know the precise ingredients in Spam, I also did not know if I was in trouble. Gram was acting all normal, but sly like the fox when the gingerbread man is on his snout.

Besides, why the hell would I be in trouble? I didn't break any laws. We weren't even doing it, weren't even that close. Then why did I feel so guilty? Then my gram, who I have decided is my new favorite person, said, "Wow. That Matt is cute." Which is so not what any teenager would actually say in a million years, but I appreciated her trying.

"I know. I think I love him a little, Gram, I really do," I said, because I wanted to share him, at least a little, with someone, and I guess the someone was going to be Gram.

I thought that she was going to hug me and say, "Oh, dahling, that's whundaful!" like Bette Davis, her eyes all shimmery, and then light up a Winston and sit down to supper. Well, she did light a cigarette. She slid a pan of Spam and tomato slices under the boiler, then she leaned against the stove. She inhaled, thinking, exhaled, thinking and frowning, and then said:

"I'm going to say this once, so listen good. Have fun. But. Just be careful. I don't want a great-grandchild. I'm too young, for Christ's sake." Then she poured two glasses of orange juice and pushed a plate of red, bubbly tomato and a charred pink square of Spam toward me. "And in a car? During the day?"

I stared at an empty plate on the kitchen table with a gray and pink starburst painted on it. It was easier to scrutinize dishes than look up at my grandma, because my cheeks were burning with mortification.

"Class it up, kid."

And because I was blushing, because I was raised right, because there was a total halo of shame around my whole body, I knew she was entirely and absolutely right.

This whole heart-to-heart was before my skulking around Dad's lair. Looking back on everything, I should have said more to Gram. The timing was perfect. But real life never gets the timing right. I could have asked her about everything she knew about my parents. I wouldn't have had to see my dad's single bed or read a letter I had no business reading. I could have gone on believing that Dad was Tiger Woods and Mom was the Virgin Mary.

But Mom's not innocent by a long shot. I'm no mathematician, but looking at some of the statements, she was slowly taking money from the D&D accounts months *before* Amanda and Dad got all reckless and disgusting. Months. She'd been planning this for ages. Premeditated theft.

Then Dad leapt into Amanda's arms and pierced navel. Because she was there, and hot. And I know from personal experience that sex or just hard-core making out is like a drug, and it can make you forget for just a short time how much life can hurt. And Dad's wife—my amazing, thieving, conniving, embezzling mother—had been leaving him slowly for months, maybe even years.

All this is too intense, like real-life-complicated-and-adult stuff.

And now I'm dizzy, remembering the night Dad moved out. Stuck on details like the shaving cream, the suitcase, Coffee. It feels like a tragedy I am reading about in a book, and also like it's happening right now. That night is *never* in the past for me. It is always happening in real time, in the present. Playing in the back of my brain on a loop.

I was standing, letting the foam slide from my skin like melted whipped cream, and then I put on a robe and went to my room.

I dragged a comb through my wet hair and lay on top of the covers. I smelled like menthol.

It was spring, a warmer night than the previous few, and raining. I listened to the drops hit the window, and I thought about nothing. My brain was in shock. Zombified. As flat and cold as porcelain.

Lightning, and thunder four, then three, then two seconds behind it.

I couldn't sleep.

After Dad left the house, gone forever, Mom stepped into my room, no knock, no nothing. She just took my hand and pulled me out of bed to the front steps of our house.

The white baselines in the baseball field across the street glowed. All summer long Little Leaguers yell "Hey batta-battabatta" from nine a.m. till dusk, but that night, it was spring and storming and silent, except for the rain and the sky illuminating with whip cracks every few minutes.

Mom didn't say anything. We sat, sheltered on the concrete porch step, watching the water come down.

The electricity in the sky was amazing.

Thick veins of neon white light ricocheted across the field. The wind was soft, the drops as fat as grapes.

And it fit us—the rain, the storm, the night. We were both damp, me from my bath, Mom from her tears, and without saying a word or even looking at each other, we both stood and held hands and ran, barefoot, screaming like maniacs across the slick black pavement to the field where we pushed our feet into the outfield grass and tossed our arms wide, spinning in circles.

We looked like happy children. We looked like Wiccan witches in our white robes, our heads thrown back to feel the rain on our faces. We looked like a mother and daughter on the eve of the Apocalypse.

It used to be an important and good memory that made me feel that it was me and Mom against the world. But after everything, in the here and now, this memory makes me feel like an accomplice. I didn't know that you could love and hate your parents totally separately *and* equally.

But you can.

And I do.

JAGGED TRAJECTORY

We share genes,
My mother and I.
Our twinned laughter chimes,
Our hair blushes pink in tandem.

The reflection stares at its source.
Distorted with lies, age,
And embezzled trusts.
You are not what you seem.

You are a selfish faux mother demanding to know
Who is the fairest?
Insisting the hunter bring back my heart.
Your integrity of convenience is useless.

Esther and me,
We two pirouette under a bell jar,
Pale ballerinas spinning in unison
Away from betrayal.

DATE: August 9
MOOD: Infinite as Space and Wise
Beyond My Freaking Years

Matt and I have indeed done things for the very first time together. Intimate things. Romantic things. I'm trying to be fair. I'm trying to forgive him by remembering how amazing he can be. When someone is stabbing you in the heart, your first instinct is to grab the murderer's wrist and pull the knife out of your chest. Same as when you are betrayed/ shocked by your beloved boyfriend's nonvirgin status. You just want to keep him the hell away from you and your innocent, trusting, and so-hot-for-him-it-can't-help-it body. But what do I really have to do here under the hundred-pound coverlet but think about the state of affairs (ha)? I have only been focusing on the physical stuff that we do because it is what seems to matter the most to me—right now, anyway.

Matt and I go on dates, lots of them, sometimes in groups and sometimes just us. We do so much together that we could write <u>The Budget Guide to Dating in Chicagoland</u> guidebook. We go to a lot of all-ages shows. We jump around in the front and then go for doughnuts afterward or for sushi or Thai or Ethiopian. We go to the movies and eat popcorn with extra butter oil. We (try to) get pierced. We bake cupcakes from box mixes and eat them while trolling YouTube for funny shit. We drive, at my insistence, to independent bookstores in Oak Park and buy books and drink coffee, and Matt wears fake hipster glasses and pretends he is as into books as I am and gives himself a white cappuccino foam mustache to make me laugh. We go to Grant Park and walk around the rose gardens and kiss during the corny light show at Buckingham Fountain. We Netflix. We Wii. He tries to put the "friend" in "boyfriend," and I love him for it.

I also love that he drags me into the real world. I'm in my head so much that I might as well pitch a pup tent in there and stay indefinitely. Matt thinks of me as a regular girl, a regular girl with a body he wants to adore. How does one say no to that? I'm not saying he is perfect. Actually, he is quite annoying and pushy and can be a real jock asshole when he wants to be, but overall, big picture, whole package? He's mine. And deep down, in his heart of hearts, a place I think of as the chocolate chewy core of a Tootsie Pop, a place where his very personhood resides devoid of gender and hormones, etc., he honestly and truly *cares* about me.

My parents were hours away from the Great Move-Out, and although I wasn't privy to the whole business, like birds before an earthquake, I sensed that it was coming. Part of me wanted to stay in the house, absorbing every last drop-let of our family that was still under "our" roof. I wanted to clock as many hours, minutes, seconds, as I could before it all metamorphosed into the home of a broken family, a single mother and her disturbed teenage daughter.

Conversely, I also wanted to be as far away from the whole thing as possible. Weird, right? I'd bum around the hallways after school, mill around the parking lot, meet Matt for impromptu early dinners just to stay out as late as I could before dragging myself to our doorway and letting myself in. Who would be home? Would there be fighting? Noisy lovemaking? Dad packing? Mom weeping? Spin the dial. Let's see what happens. I had a recurring nightmare that I'd arrive home exhausted and homesick to find Amanda in an apron, pearls, and high heels saying, "Keek! You're just in time for *supper*!"

So the Saturday that Dad moved out, I was on the fence about going to the Art Institute with Matt. It would be a whole day away. I had begun to think of myself as my par-ents' babysitter. Who the hell knew what they would get up to without my constant surveillance? They might eat the poison under the sink or stick bobby pins in light sockets.

Matt's parents were museum members, so it was a cheap date and I'm into art. Who isn't? "It'll be good for you," Matt said. "We might even have fun. I'll get you a latte in the din-ing room." And he looked at me like I was a little kid whose puppy had just gotten hit by a car and he would do anything to cheer me up.

Chicago loves tourists. There are hundreds of thousands of them at the Art Institute on any Saturday, and they all stand in front of Seurat's *A Sunday Afternoon on the Island of La Grande Jatte*. They take pictures of it, and then they get real close to see all the dots. And then they go to see the Renoirs, the van Goghs, the Monets, and the Picassos.

Okay, it is perhaps the most impressive art museum in the world. But when you grow up going there, the tourists from Japan and Germany and Ontario, the security guards staring you down, the art safari mentality of everyone visiting—it kind of gets on your nerves. My favorite is *Nighthawks*, the Hopper painting of the diner, because it reminds me of getting coffee at Dunkin' Donuts on Clark and Belmont with the Squirrel and Matt. I am the woman in the red dress. I love Gustave Caillebotte's *Paris Street; Rainy Day* because it is so gigantic you feel like you are on the street in Paris, and everyone seems a little depressed and has an umbrella, like they are all under their own little bell jars, and looking at it makes my heart sprout little wings. The painting is so good, it is like reading a book in one glance. So, right off the bat Matt and I went to see my two favorite paintings, and then I let him pick where he wanted to go.

That day was overcast, and the whole museum seemed melancholy. Matt and I usually talked when we were out in the city, if not about anything important, at least about whatever was happening at the museum or bookstore or restaurant. That Saturday I didn't feel like saying anything about anything. And Matt didn't push it. We walked through the museum as solemn as undertakers, holding hands, Matt pulling me forward a little to the exhibit he wanted to see, and me just going along with it. I thought he might go all *Ferris Bueller's Day Off* and take me to the Chagall windows to make out, but he didn't. Then I thought he might take me to see the Diane Arbus photographs in the basement, but although he knows me pretty well, he is not a mind reader.

American Gothic? Warhol's *Mao?* He took me, of course, to *trumpet fanfare* the Arthur Rubloff paperweight collection(?), which I thought was the lamest and most ridiculous idea ever and exactly the kind of jock-brained notion he would have.

The paperweights were in a small dark gallery, but each globe was a little world of sparkle flowers, each shiny and liquidy like delicious hard candies for a god from outer space. They were dazzling, reflecting off mirrored shelves. Tourists were not that into them, so it was calm and library-quiet. Matt and I had decided not to talk at all by that point and instead mimed our delight and interest with wide eyes and broad head nods. We held hands tightly as we peered at a whole series of coiled snake paperweights, which were miraculous. Green snakes, black-and-yellow-striped snakes on gravel, totally realistic and creepy.

According to the wall copy, glass paperweights became popular in the 1800s when the postal service got dependable and everyone started writing letters like crazy. People needed the weights to keep their papers together. I could so use one now to keep *my* pages together. Funny how my life is.

So there we were, holding hands, looking at these paperweights, and I wasn't thinking of anything in particular, just staring at the beautiful objects, when suddenly Matt was wiping my face with his hands and flicking tears from my checks with his long wrestler-calloused fingers.

I was crying and wasn't even aware of it. There were no words that I wanted to say, so I just closed my eyes to force the tears to flow from behind my lids, my tears and the glass globes all made of the same watery translucence. I could feel my heart beating apart from everyone else's, whispering *IamIamIam* just like Esther's in times of great existential distress. And I am. And I am separate from everything and connected to all, and it was all so overwhelming, no wonder my tears were splashing like rain.

Matt did indeed buy me a latte. And a slice of flourless chocolate cake. We never talked about my miniature breakdown at the Art Institute. What was I crying about? Everything. I was mourning everything—my family, my childhood. I think that maybe I was also mourning the end of

Matt and me, which was sure to come, eventually, whether I slept with him or not. In that little room I felt time pressing on me, squeezing me like a piece of coal, turning me into a diamond, and it hurt like hell. Forever to his credit, Matt stood tall and held my hand.

We sat on the top tier passenger seats of the Metra on the way home, staring down at the city and suburbs swimming past the green windows as if we were fish watching from inside an aquarium. And we were swimming, treading water until everything came to a stop.

IamIamIam.

DATE: August 10
MOOD: Juvenile Delinquent

I've been hearing the ice-cream truck in my grandma's neighborhood cranking out "Do Your Ears Hang Low?" every summer since I was born. When I was a kid, Gram or Dad or Mom would give me a dollar, and I'd run like a girl escaping a fire down the front steps and up to the window of the Good Humor van. Which is so George Orwell's <u>1984</u>, a government van that dispenses happy dispositions: Dreamsicles. King Cones. PushUps. Today when I heard it, I grabbed a handful of silver change from Gram's dresser and ran to meet the truck like it was a long-lost friend.

The EPA needs to investigate the ozone-depleting exhalations of the Chicagoland fleet of ice-cream trucks. It was hot enough without the truck idling, its exhaust blasting the ankles of all the kids waiting for their ice-cream novelties. A plump boy in front bought an astro pop while I looked at the pictures of ice cream. I so should have asked him who he was before he was born, but I wasn't thinking. The ice-cream man was out of everything I wanted, so I somehow ended up with Dora the Explorer. On a stick.

Instead of going inside I sat on the front steps, giving my pox scars a chance to absorb the sun and watching summer unfold in the street. Down the block, girls drew on the sidewalk with fat sticks of chalk. Boys, top heavy in helmets, zoomed around, their bikes pimped out with bells and training wheels. Teenagers I didn't know drove by with their windows down, stupid pop music pulsing from crappy speakers. Dora's hair was strawberry-flavored, though I remembered it as chocolate. She was a fast melter, and I had to concentrate to keep up.

For a minute everything was good. It was August. My chicken pox were gone. My boyfriend and I were working it out. I was young, you know? The world was my freaking oyster. My extraordinary little cousin was healthy-ish at last. Mom the Embezzler was coming home soon. I didn't know what the hell I would say to her, but she would be home at least. And things might seem a little more normal, whatever normal was for us. I was thinking that whatever went on between my parents had absolutely nothing to do with me, and for the first time ever, really, I believed it. For the first time in about a hundred years, everything was okay.

And then I saw *her*.

I let one of Dora's sad, melty eyeballs roll out of her face and down the steps.

She looked the same as she did making change at the D&D. She wore a double tank top and a knit miniskirt and flip-flops. It was summer, and she looked practically naked. She carried a giant Big Gulp cup from the 7-Eleven around the corner, and as she neared my grandma's house, she knocked the ice against the cup sides with a nervous flick of her wrist. I knew she was there to see if Dad was around, and duh, he was w-o-r-k-i-n-g to help fix the whole train wreck of our lives.

I pretended I didn't see her, my heart doing jumping jacks in my chest. I turned my head and tried to finish the rest of Dora so I didn't look like an even more pathetic and underage loser virgin than I already was. I chewed the remaining black gum eyeball. I thought of the talks we'd had over the dishwasher, and the pretend smoking out back, and how much I once loved her. I imagined calling her Mom, as in "stepmom," and almost keeked.

"Dad's not here." I was staring straight out across the street, looking at chalk butterflies and rainbows glowing up from the pavement. "So piss off."

I sounded totally tough, right? But I wanted to flee the scene. I wanted to run and keep going until I was somewhere safe and quiet where I could think. Her sunglasses were totally cool and covered half her face with black lenses. I couldn't help but notice that her toenails were painted Lincoln Park After Dark purple-black.

"I'm not here to see Kevin." Amanda slurped up melted ice from her stupid Big Gulp, which is perhaps the most inelegant sound in the universe. For a minute I was like, *Who the hell is Kevin?* And duh, I know who the hell he is. Was she freaking showing off that she calls my *father* Kevin? That they are *peers, sexual partners, "lovers"*?

On reality shows and soap operas and, once in a blue moon, even on *Judge Judy*, women become so inflamed with hatred, jealousy, and anger that, before you can say "Order in the court," they are at each other's throats, pulling out hair like wolverines, and doing the girl fight dance while the cameras try to catch it all. It always seemed childish to me. I would never debase myself in such a way. But as Amanda stood there, a veil of red descended across my vision, and I wanted to bash her head against the sidewalk and hopscotch over her limp body.

Sometimes when I get really agitated or nervous or excited, the muscles beneath my clavicles shudder under my skin like the flanks of a racehorse. They were shuddering, and my hands were shaking, and I didn't know what I was supposed to do. Gram had just told me to class it up, and I wasn't about to go all Roller Derby on her in the middle of the street, so I held my breath and let sweat drip down my temples, hoping that I could somehow fast-forward to the part where I'm an adult looking back on this.

"I'm here to see you. Matt gave me the address. He's

worried about you, kid." Now she was talking to *Matt*? "He told me about the chicken pox too."

HUH?

"I bumped into him and Earl when I was picking up my last check from the D&D. Matt was kind of an asshole to me, actually. I deserve it, I guess."

God, I love him.

"He told me that I should say something to you about everything. That I owed you that. Here." She handed me a white paper bag from the D&D that I hadn't noticed she was carrying. "I thought you should have these, give you something to do while you get better."

The bag was heavy, and inside were bottles of nail polish. All the subversive ones we'd bought together and some she'd shoplifted from Sephora, back when we were the best of friends. They were all there, the whole gang: Off with Her Red, Jade Is the New Black, Damsel in a Dress. We're talking, like, seventy-five dollars' worth. I was excited at the bonanza. And furious that I was excited. And had to stifle an urge to take each bottle out one by one and fling it onto the pavement so they exploded in Technicolor bombs.

Amanda still hadn't said anything worthwhile. And I wasn't about to say "Thank you, you skank, for giving me used nail polish in a bag from my parents' restaurant."

"How are you, anyway?"

IhateyouIhateyouIhateyouIhate: YOU. And then I said,

"Why don't you find some other person's life to demolish? There are plenty of nice innocent children all around here. I'm sure their dads would be happy to fuck your brains out."

Good, right? Do not mess with the Keekinator. The blow landed hard, because she actually gasped and took a slight step backward. I couldn't see her eyes, but her Big Gulp cup was suddenly sofa king still.

"It's not like that, Keek. Your dad's cool and everything, but what we did, it wasn't important, really. I mean, we were a little drunk and a lot lonely." She had obviously scripted this at home. "I wasn't thinking about anything. It was totally and completely stupid. I mean, we're not in love or anything."

Oh, Esther Greenwood. WTF am I supposed to say now?

"I will never forgive you," is what I said. As solemn and pale as Wednesday Addams.

"I never meant to hurt you, you know. It wasn't a big elaborate plan to ruin your life." Which was actually extremely good to hear. "We were just adults behaving badly. If I could undo it, I would. Your dad is even more upset than I am."

"Really?"

"Your mom and him—whoa. I'm no therapist, but they should not be married."

I'm totally paraphrasing all of this, but that was the gist of her intended communiqué. But then I said, and this is pretty much verbatim:

"Yeah. I know. But I thought you were my friend. Or at least on my team, Amanda. It wouldn't hurt so much if it were anyone but you. *Anyone.* Like any other person in the whole freaking world, even my English teacher, and I am serious." And I was breathing hard and suddenly dripping wet with sweat, and I said, "Thanks for the chitchat and the nail polish, but we are so over."

And as I stood to go inside, she said in a normal and as-serious-as-I've-ever-heard-it voice, "I'm really sorry, Karina." Finally. The she-wolf apologizes.

"Yeah, well. You *are* sorry. Now get off my stairs."

Cue lights and music. Keek has left the building. I went inside and sat on the couch, nervously shaking the bag so the bottles *click-clock*ed together, watching her out the picture window like the final frames of a movie as she turned and slowly walked down the block to wherever she'd parked her crappy hatchback.

Coming here had taken guts, I guess. I suppose I should have appreciated it, but I didn't. Or at least I didn't just then. I felt like I'd handled the whole confrontation like a sophisticated person. And I was feeling a tiny bit better, calmer even. I went to the bathroom in a daze, thinking about how young I'd been three months before, three weeks, three minutes—how old I felt just then. How before I knew it, I would be at college, on my own. Washing my hands, I thought about how I'll be taking Driver's Ed. in the fall. I have a cousin so much younger than me that she will probably call me Auntie just to be polite. I was feeling what my mom's guru would have called "the serenity that only emotional growth and wisdom can bring." And then I looked into the mirror, and my entire mouth was black and purple from the stupid Dora gum, and I looked like a crazy witch girl, with black teeth and black and pink hair. I'd been talking to Amanda the whole time with this mouth of ridiculousness.

Sofa.

King.

Pathetic.

Ugh.

DATE: August 12
MOOD: Sunkissed and Glowy

Dad took me to the beach yesterday.

I was surprised he took the day off work and even took the magnetic Dine & Dash signs off the van. When I was a kid we used to go to the beach often, and I'd forgotten how great it was. But I hadn't packed my suit when I'd gotten sick, duh, and he didn't have any of our beach stuff—umbrella, blanket, sunscreen. So on the way downtown, we swung by the house, and when I say "house," I mean his old, my and Mom's current, abode.

Awk.

Ward.

Mom had changed the locks, and only I had a key. "Wait here," I said, and went in, like we were pulling off a bank robbery. I couldn't think about what he was thinking, fiddling with the XM Radio controls while I entered the forbidden zone.

The house was still and airless. Coffee's water bowl was empty. The digital clock on the microwave had the correct time. This house had just been sitting here the whole time I'd been gone, and it totally creeped me out. I felt like any minute I was going to discover a body splayed out on the living room floor with a steak knife sticking out of his chest, or drug dealers hiding in the mudroom with wires taut between their hands, waiting to strangle me. It was my house but fundamentally different. It was a house and not a home. I'd always heard there was a difference, but only then did I understand what people who said that were getting at.

I grabbed a bathing suit from my top drawer, took off all my clothes, pulled on the suit (a black one-piece with two silver rings at the hips), and then put my clothes back on over it. It was like having on a superhero costume. At the first cry for help I could tear off my clothes and fly to the rescue—<u>Bell Jar</u> Girl. Saving lives through difficult and genre-bending poetry.

A sheet, a bottle of Coppertone, and towels from the closet, an umbrella from the garage, and I was back in the van so fast even my dad, in his slightly preoccupied frame of mind, was surprised.

I didn't tell Dad about Amanda's visit, because really it had nothing to do with him. I don't feel sorry for my dad. He is an adult. He has the benefit of experience, which gives him access to wisdom, right? He still is one infuriating man, but if he's trying, I suppose I should too.

"Okay," I said. "Let's go." To get to the expressway Dad had to take the same route as he would to drive to the D&D for the first few miles. He had been navigating this way toward the restaurant for almost ten years. He could have driven the route with his eyes closed, at least till we got to the Eisenhower. But yesterday his eyes were wide open, like he was taking it all in for the very last time. For Christ's sake. Weren't we supposed to be having fun? And so I started to sing "The Beautiful Sea" in total Ethel Merman, jazz hands, child star of vaudeville mode, even though it's, um, a lake. And it dawned on me at that moment that I was sofa king determined to make him happy that it was ridiculous.

But it worked. Dad joined in, singing in a dooby, dooby, doo Sinatra-esque fashion. Then we listened to the oldies channel, driving on the expressway until the suburbs disappeared and we were surrounded by skyscrapers and giant billboards and we were at Oak Street Beach.

We parked and dragged our crap from the van. We walked past hot dog vendors over fiery hot sand to a spot close to the water and unfurled our sheet between a Mexican family and a gay couple.

Dad opened the giant umbrella and poked the spike into the sand like he was harpooning a whale or raising the flag at Iwo Jima. His every motion felt important and camera ready: Divorced Man Takes His Only and Troubled Daughter to the Beach.

Me, I was just trying to keep the sun from getting onto my skin without my permission. Ozone layer, global warming, etc. In layman's terms, I fry. It took me twenty minutes to slather the SPF 50 over every inch. As I rubbed the lotion across my legs and arms, neck, face, the holes in the silver rings, I could feel where there once had been chicken pox.

Meanwhile, on the other side of the sheet, Dad took off his shoes and pushed his socks into them. Then he took off his shirt. He was tall and lean, but some forlorn hairs on his skinny chest were gray. His shorts had tiki flames on them and were way too young for him. Surf's up, dude. Gnarly midlife crisis. Bitchin' mess your life is. And before I could join him, he yelled, "Rotten egg!" and bounded into the water like a deranged golden retriever.

Unbelievable, these adults. Just when you think their actions are predictable, just when you think you know them inside and out and understand how they see the world, how you fit into it, and what they expect of you, they up and change. I wanted to run after him, splash around and cool off and just play with my dad in the water. I wanted it to be like when I was little and he called me jelly bean when I wore a bathing suit because I looked like one. I'm not a jelly bean anymore.

Make no mistake, I'm still furious at him.

I burn easily.

Besides, I couldn't just leave all our stuff alone. So I

scrunched back farther into the shade of the umbrella, opened up my copy of The Bell Jar to the beach scene and read words I could have recited by memory as my Dad's head bobbed up and down in the faraway waves.

Before I'd known we were going to the beach, I had taken all of the nail polishes Amanda had given me as a parting gift and I'd painted each finger and toe a different color. The overall tone of them was dark, so it wasn't like a rainbow of craziness on my extremities. My fingertips looked like I'd slammed them in a car door and left them to throb—black, purple, green, and blue. Same with my feet, and I buried my toes in the sand, hoping that some of the polish would wear off quicker. I had decided to use my nails as a timer for getting over Amanda. I would not use acetone remover. I would wait for the polish to chip and wear away on its own, bit by bit, each square of paint eroding a little more every day. When all the polish was gone, Amanda would be out of my system for real. That was the Einsteinian plan, anyway.

When you are mad at your dad for sleeping with a so-called friend of yours, your family is disintegrating before your very eyes, and you are recovering from a nasty bout of the chicken pox, do not set your blanket up between the world's most adorable family and the most in-love gay couple in all of Chicago. The family was a mom, a dad, an older boy who was about six, and a little girl who was about four. They'd brought tacos and orange soda. They played with a beach ball. The father buried the boy in the sand. The daughter made castles with a yellow plastic castle mold. They were happy the whole time. They took turns swimming. They smiled. A lot.

The other guys were in their twenties. They spread sunscreen on each other's backs. They played chess on a travel chessboard. On the beach! They laughed frequently. Although they didn't kiss or make out in any way, their knees or hands or feet were always casually touching. They were totally together. Totally happy. And I was about to fall asleep, I was so depressed and warm and lulled by the waves and the gulls and the *thump-click* of chess pieces and giggles of family harmony and my heart beating *IamIamIam*.

Then Dad lumbered across the sand and crash-landed on the sheet spraying water everywhere. *Ka-thunk*. And he saw: the family. He saw: the couple. He lay down and closed his eyes. I couldn't tell if it was water or sweat or what, but some kind of liquid rolled from his eyes to the sheet, and he sighed and said, "Keek?"

And I said, "Yeah?"

His skin was very white. He didn't look old-old, but he looked older than he had three months ago. I wanted to put a pillow under his head, drape a blanket across him like he was sick and I was there to take care of him, instead of the other way around. Droplets of water sparkled on his collarbone, then evaporated.

Just when I thought he was asleep, his breathing regular and his body still, he said, "I love you. And if you never forgive me, I will still love you anyway and will still be your dad. No matter what."

I didn't say anything. I was thinking of something to say to let him know I was still really pissed without swearing or saying something I would later regret. I thought of phrases from this book I got for an essay I wrote for English on *The Taming of the Shrew* about international insults, and these were my options:

1. Up yours!
2. You and your mother, too!
3. You bastard!
And my favorite
4. Go piss up a rople!

None of which were entirely appropriate. I still said nothing, and he said, "You want a hot dog? Come on, I'll get you a hot dog."

And suddenly, despite my quasi meat boycott, our ability to eat all the hot dogs our hearts could ever desire at the D&D, and my avoidance of *El Sol*, I found myself standing up and saying, "Okay, Dad. I'll eat a hot dog with you. Least I could do." I asked the couple to watch our things. We hopped/walked to the sidewalk, risking our lives by crossing the path for Rollerbladers, skaters, and cyclists, to get beach dogs.

The Chicago beach hot dog is an entirely different species of dog from the Chicago-style hot dog of lore. Its bun is not seeded. The hot dog itself is naked but for a swipe of brown mustard. It is not wrapped in paper but tucked into a silver envelope that says HOT DOG in blue letters. There is something about the fresh lake air, the sun bouncing off the skyscrapers, the seagulls circling like buzzards, the extra tang of sand that inevitably finds its way into the last bite, that makes the beach dog the king of Chicago Hot Dogs. I guess it's a local thing. An entry for the Not for Tourists Guide.

I don't know if I have mentioned that my dad and I used to be—if not best friends before all this nonsense began—at least really friendly lab partners. I could always count on him for important things. To know when and how to do the right thing in most situations. But this situation is beyond what I ever thought would have happened to us. I see now that this whole beach date is how we will repair things. For the rest of my life I will date my father on the weekends. We will go to movies, to dinner, to roller-coaster parks, and exhibitions at the Museum of Science and Industry. He will take me to breakfast at the *Chicago Tribune*'s top-ten places for breakfast in Chicago. Afterward we will browse bookstores on the North Side. On nice days we will go to the Lincoln

Park Zoo, Navy Pier, the Botanic Garden. He will become a different kind of boyfriend. He is my dad, and I love him, whether I can forgive him or not.

Life is freaking impossible. Mom comes home on Monday. I gotta pack and whatever.

Yes sir, yes sir, one bag full.

DATE: August 13
MOOD: There's No Place Like Om

When Mom picked me up from Gram's today, we had set up a fire alarm system. She said she would call Gram's number, let it ring once, and then hang up. How KGB. Then I was supposed to sling my bag over my shoulder, kiss Gram on the cheek, and head out the door when Mom's car pulled up in front of the house.

During my illness, I watched a PBS show where they removed a rotten tooth from a lion that was heavily sedated at some Australian zoo. It was quick and painless, and the dentist was in and out in minutes. This is how the pickup would have gone, but for some reason when we did it, the lion woke the hell up. First off, Dad was home, which was news to us all. He practically answered the phone before it rang. "Huh. That's weird," he said when there was no one on the other end. So I had to tell him that Mom was coming to pick me up. "Oh, good, I'd like to talk with her," he said. Which was the whole reason for the subterfuge in the first place.

Duh.

Mom told me that she was just a little burnt out from her trip to "deal with your father on top of everything else." And although I sort of knew what she meant, I'd just started "dealing with" my father again, and he wasn't so horrible, really.

So when Mom pulled up, instead of me slipping off into the sunset, pox-free and 10 pounds thinner, my dad lumbered down the porch steps before me and stood leaning into the driver's side window like a flirting teenager, talking about God knows what with his soon-to-be ex-wife.

Then Gram waltzed into the front room and lit up a Winston, and we just stood there watching the real-life drama unfold. Reality unscripted is actually a little boring. They just talked. I thought there would be screaming and shouting. Perhaps pounding on the car roof. I turned away from the window and sat on the radiator cover and looked at my gram.

"Well, kid," she said. "I guess this is good-bye." She said it just like that actor from that movie in the desert with the war and the Nazis, and we both had a short chuckle. She looked good. I imagined her in a dress with shoulder pads and a 1940s hairdo like the tattooed lady who pierced Matt had. I felt like whatever was coming, at least I had her in all my scenes, four inches taller in her peep-toe platform sandals.

"Thanks for everything, Gram. I mean, it was fun—in between the puking and blood and Spam and everything." And I meant it. I didn't really want to go home. The last time I was there, I felt like the house was going to murder me. I missed my dog, my room, YouTube, etc., but here, I'd had a little room of my own and a typewriter, and a place to think that wasn't dripping with memories of happy familydom. I mean, at Gram's I wrote, like, hundreds of pages. Amazing! Who knew I had it in me?

Gram is a woman of few words. She hugged me, and we were both a little sad. And then she said, "Go on down there. They are your parents. Not much you can do about it." Right before I opened the door, she said, "Wait a minute," and then she came back with the IBM typewriter. "Keep it. It's yours. Let me help you down with it." So she took one half, I took the other, and we crab-walked it to the backseat of Mom's car. Gram and Mom waved/smiled/shot laser beams through their eyes at each other, and I waved at my dad and got into the car.

During the drive Mom patted my hand every now and again and blathered on and on about Aurora this and Aurora that, and "You look great. Hard to believe you were ever sick. Dad says you went to the beach? Great." And blah, and blah, and blah. I stared at the yellow lines in the center of the road until we were out of Gram and Dad's neighborhood and well on the way to our own.

I was so overcome with daughterly joy at seeing my long-lost embezzling mother that for the first three miles or so I was simply content. It seemed, there in the passenger seat, that everything was the way it was supposed to be. Back to normal. How it was before Dad moved out, Mom went to California, and I got the chicken pox. As right as freaking rain. Then we passed this motel with the diving girl on the 1960s VACANCY sign.

The girl is a very simple design. She has no face, wears a red bathing suit and a white bathing cap, and is folded in half in a dive position. This is to denote that the motel has a pool. When I was a kid looking out the window driving home from Gram's house, I never saw the girl diving. To me it always looked like a pork chop or T-bone steak, like her white bathing cap and the white space where she was bent in two was a bone, and the red suit was meat, and her pink arms and legs, gristle. And then one night, for some reason I looked at the sign and recognized the girl as a girl. In a white cap and red bathing suit. Diving. And try and try and try as I might, I cannot for the life of me ever see her as a piece of steak again. It's like my whole perspective has changed and there's nothing I can do about it but keep moving.

And so it is with my dear sweet self-absorbed fraud-committing mother.

Overnight she somehow morphed from a dizzy, artistic woman-wronged entrepreneur into a diabolical she-devil-alien-mom. As the wheels purred over newly poured summer blacktop, the muscles beneath my clavicles started to quiver and shake, and before I could think to take a deep breath, count to ten, or bide my time until we were in the house, I clenched my fists into angry mallets and pounded the car roof, screaming, "How could you do it? To our family!" And then I got supercreepy quiet. "For Christ's sake. Why?"

Why I didn't ask my dad that, I'm not sure. I think it has something to do with us being women, like there is a total sisterhood code and she broke it by lying to me. Same with Amanda.

Not that Dad was an angel or anything. I'm probably in for years of therapy because of his behavior. I will be like Esther Greenwood with Dr. Nolan, going on and on about my father this, and Daddy that, and "Time's up. Let's begin here next session." Dad was just being an asshole, and besides, we had our talk. Dad and I were on the road to being cool with each other, at least. At the very least, Dad was trying.

This woman driving the car? She had a lot of explaining to do.

And if we had been the magnificent friends Mom always said we were, she would have talked with me about her plans, and I would have talked her out of it, and then perhaps Mom, Dad, and I would all be driving home together now, planning a trip to the Wisconsin Dells.

Instead I was sitting at a stoplight, looking through my window at the motel sign, desperately searching for a pork chop, waiting for an answer. And this is what she said:

"I was trapped, Keek. There was nothing else I could do. If there was, I would have, but there wasn't." Then she leaned forward and rested her forehead against the steering wheel. The air-conditioning blew a tiny pink braid back from her temple, revealing its gray roots. "I'm so fucking sorry." Then she started to cry, and the light went green, and angry horns beeped, and we were off.

"Yeah, well," I said.

"Besides, Keek," she said, sniffling and getting her Zen on. "This really is between your dad and me, our development, and our growth. Amanda was collateral damage. Your dad's forgiven me. So lighten up. You and Matt have stuff that's just between you. And Dad and I have stuff that's just between us."

"Don't compare Matt and me to you and Dad, or I'm going to puke right here on the floor mat. That is sofa king ridiculous, Mom."

"And don't 'sofa king' me, Keek. In the mood for this, I am not."

Whatever, Yoda. I just wanted to be back in my own bed.

"Dad could have pressed charges, you know. Still can. Should." Have I *ever* talked this way to my mother? There was something dangerous about it, the power I was feeling, like I was inhaling frozen white light and it was darting from my mouth in sharp, icy stabs straight at her heart. I felt out of control. Possessed—aka really good.

"He wouldn't." But she looked scared for a minute, swerving a little as we neared our intersection.

"That's his apology about Amanda, I guess, not getting the police involved," I said, as if saying it out loud made it the truth. "And your pink braid is sofa king stupid."

My mom smirked, and then we were pulling into our driveway and I let her help me inside with the typewriter and my bag full of clean clothes and the box of vintage wonders from Gram.

Everyone is wrong and everyone is right and we are alive, so there you go. Mom had picked up Coffee earlier, so now I'm in my old room listening to her toenails clicking across the kitchen linoleum. I'm a little sick of words tonight, but still. I'm sitting here, typing and typing and typing because I'm like, now what? I haven't even told Matt I'm back. An alien with a similar personality to my mother's has inhabited her suit of skin and is walking around the house crumbling dog food into Coffee's dish and making instant iced tea. And I'm still fuming, smoldering mad at her, and I still love her more than I perhaps ever have because I have seen a side of her that is new to me. And this will feel better one fine day, but that is not today.

Thank God for Sylvia Plath and her <u>Bell Jar</u> world. It cheers me up. It emboldens me. It helps me interpret my own life experiences so that I start to believe that I am—if not wise, then at least more capable of handling my screwed-up life. That I'm not alone.

As I type and reread and type and reread these last weeks, I see this whole time as a kind of fever dream. I remember it all in ultra-vivid detail: cannibal cups, Hershey, Amanda and Dora gumballs, Judge Judy, Muguet Des Bois, Matt's mouth, Dad's tiki flames, Gram and her shock treatment and vintage secrets, Nic and the Squirrel, the pox and the blood, all of it, everything. And one day, maybe I'll forget the excruciatingly painful specifics but the truth is, all of these experiences—good, bad, and otherwise—are part of me now. Like my bones, my pox scars, the holes that pierce my ears. What is done cannot be undone. There's nothing I can do but what Gram said, put my head down and just get on with it.

Esther Greenwood comes to the same conclusion. And not long after, she is free to go, to walk right out of the asylum and start her real and true life all over again, as if she never went crazy and never tried to off herself.

She gets a second chance. So do Mom and Dad. And me, I suppose, to recover from everything.

And now that I'm here—back home, or whatever you want to call this place where I grew up with two parents—I'm wondering how much recent events have damaged my psyche. Gram said I would survive and she was right. What else is there to do? I mean, yeah, I got the mumps and chicken pox within six months of each other, dyed my hair black and pink, toyed with the idea of getting my tongue pierced and giving it up to Matt, but when all is said and done, I'm really, like, fine. Okay for now. It's a little anticlimactic. No heads in ovens. No asylum roommates. No shock therapy or medication. Just okay.

I'm sitting in my room, cross-legged on the floor, and it's silent but for the *clackity-clack* of the typewriter keys and that old brag of my heart. *IamIamIam*. It beats. And that is totally what my heart is doing all the time: *bragging*. Showing off, boasting about how good it is at keeping me alive. My heart's a prizefighter, expecting the best from me at all times. And there is always, at the end of the day, just—me.

Existing is not quite enough. Passionate living is the best revenge.

Which is why, despite the demoralizing events of late, I am still thrilled about Aurora. She's living and not dying anymore. Mom left her digital camera on the kitchen table and I beeped through the pictures. They went from Aurora lying in an incubator like a chicken breast in a microwave to a video of her at home in a purple Onesie, sucking like crazy on a bedazzled pacifier.

Aurora is beautiful. I'm not *into* babies or anything, but I've been the only kid in my entire family for forever, and I'm not really a kid anymore. And when she's older and can talk, I can say, "Oh, when you were born, I had the chicken pox. It was the hottest summer in Chicago, and the whole time I languished in my grandma's spare bedroom, I just knew that you would be absolutely fine. And here, I wrote a poem all about it."

AURORA

Shhhhh
Breath over teeth to whisper you
Into the world.
You're too early.
We're not ready.
Hold on.
Translucent sea creature sleeping,
Delicate and rosy-fingered
Body curled into a fist
An oyster clutching a pearl.
You, exquisite and vulnerable—
Technology was made for you.

DATE: September 22
MOOD: Centered

Closure. I'm kind of into it, seeing as there's not much of it in real life. I think it is what we seek in great literature. I was in my room, pulling together supplies for school, when—lo and behold—there was my whole stack of tea-stained and dog-eared sheets of heartbreak from my <u>Bell Jar</u> summer. All lovingly held together with three bulldog clips.

And I realized that I had to at least finish it.

I'm not going to work on this for the rest of my life. There's got to be a beginning, middle, and end, and this is it. The end, I mean. Taking a break from typing was good. Stepping back and really living was awesome. Going garage sailing with Nic and the Squirrel, going to the Music Box Theatre's animation festival, barbecuing marinated tofu slabs in Matt's backyard. The last three weeks of summer in Keekville were superb. Not so much with the parents' marriage, but things are not as blindingly depressing as they were a month ago.

For one thing, school has started. And believe me, school

is *the* great distracter. I think people can tell that I have been through some major shit, but they don't say anything. They just seem to look at me and see me, which is different from how it was in June. And it is good to be recognized for me and not as the resident psycho or the hot wrestler's girlfriend.

Nic and I are still cool. Thank God. She cut my hair. She said, "The only statement this hair is making is, 'I am insane,'" and she took scissors she bought at Sally's Beauty Supply and cut it into a flapper-y bob. And then she doused my head in "Chestnut" (what, had I been in the marketing department of L'Oréal, would have been christened "Love You a Latte"). And, voila! With a lot of pomade and curls at cheek height, I look like Dorothy Parker's badass little sister. Nic and I are dedicating four weekend hours to creating masterpieces for our Etsy shop. The rest are earmarked for whatshisname—oh, yes, the love of my life, Mutant Frogboy himself, Matt.

Oh, virginity! You temptress! I think I am firmly—at least until Matt's junior prom, anyway—staying away from that bridge. As you know, I think about it all the time. And I mean a lot. And I have come to the conclusion, having read the evidence laid out so clearly on these very pages, that I am not ready to go there, yet. I am ready to dip a toe into the water. I am willing to taste the water, scooping my hand in and sipping from my palm like a clever gorilla at a mountain stream. I run around all day with my bathing suit under my clothes just in case I decide to go swimming—and yet, I am not prepared (as of this writing) to take the proverbial *plunge*. And so we will continue to look, lick, kiss, caress, and basically do everything but. And that is really okay with me, and it is really okay with Matt. And I believe him when he says it is really okay. And if it's not, all I have to do is think of my cool Gram and my own trajectory, and tell him to go piss up a rope.

Not having the chicken pox? Glorious!

Parents not skulking around acting all depressed and confusing and infuriating? Grand!

Having Nic back as my real-life pal? *Wunderbar!*

Amanda moving to Minneapolis? Best idea ever!

Matt getting a parking space in the junior lot? Hot!

One day, when I am choosing a dress to wear to the Pulitzer Prize awards ceremony, thinking of what to say in my acceptance speech, I must remember to mention my humble beginnings as the—are you sitting down?—managing poetry editor of *Ctl. Alt. Delete*, my school's brand-new literary magazine.

I know!

The newspaper was so not up my alley. The five *W*s of irrelevance:

Who? Homecoming king and queen.

What? Homecoming.

Where? The gym.

When? Mid-October.

Why? Who the hell knows.

No, thanks.

You can't have any significant leadership role in any school organization as a sophomore. However, a recommendation from one or two honors English teachers and a submission of a poem or two (*from these very pages*) and Scholastic Art and Writing Award, here I come! How Sylvia Plathian! That, Algebra II, and letting my hair grow out is giving me good 'n' plenty to think about besides *le divorce*. Most of the time.

Let me be clear. My life is still, er, challenging. Every once in a while a feeling of great sadness and despair overcomes me. They say that when epileptics have seizures, sometimes they have a weird vision in their head, like a bear riding a bicycle in the corner of their eye. Or they smell a nonexistent smell like gasoline or burnt toast, and that's how they know that, in any minute, they are going to go into spasms and flop around on the floor and freak out everyone in the room/auditorium/roller-coaster line/restaurant.

I don't have seizures, but sometimes I feel <u>The Bell Jar</u> hovering over me a little, like a spaceship tracking my every move. When I sense it coming, any little thing can set me off. If I come across some old shirts my dad forgot to take out of the back of his closet, or if I find a dried-up bottle of nail polish in the bottom of a reusable shopping bag in the trunk of Matt's car, or if I see my mom looking at me as if I am a person she has never met before in her life—I'll lose it and have to sit on my bed, on a chair, behind a closed bathroom stall door. I hold my head in my hands, listen to that old freaking brag of my heart, and let the tears fall where they may, before standing up and getting back out there.

But this is a thousand pounds better than I was before.

At least I'm not dry-heaving anxiety into garbage cans in homeroom.

In other more pressing real-world news, Dad got himself a business partner, some guy he went to college with who has an MBA, so the D&D is in good shape, which is important to me, because it's the only thing that hasn't totally changed in the last year. And its profit will pay for college and Dad's rent for his—drum roll, please—new apartment. Which is not far from the Dine & Dash. Furniture by IKEA. Styling by Keek. I have a room there with a little blue writing desk that Nic and I scored from a garage sail. Dad calls it the Virginia Woolf room. It is really a breakfast nook with an IKEA room divider as a door, but it's mine, and I can stay there when I want and bring my laptop there when I want, and it's another place to be besides home, or rather, another home. In addition to the one I inhabit with *her*.

She is, actually, not so bad. Annoying and really into the white wine, but also really taking herself and her parenting responsibilities way more seriously than I can ever remember.

For instance, she signed us up for mother-daughter pottery lessons at this new shop that opened in our neighborhood. It's called Works of Earth, and at first I was all eye rolling and aggravated because it was ridiculous. Most of the daughters were ten. The teacher is a total hippy, like, crunch, crunch, crunch. He walks among the wheels in his clogs humming and saying things like "Communicate with the clay," "Center," and—my favorite—"Breathe through your belly," as if that is where the lungs are.

The first day, Mom made a bowl you could totally eat cereal out of, while I couldn't even slap the clay on the wheel right. But we're at week four now, and I'm sort of into it. My mom is into our teacher. By the time this session is over, I'm sure she and Mr. Crunch will be dating, whatever that means. It probably means yoga classes, foreign films, wine tastings, art openings in crappy suburban galleries. Despite my wariness of my mother's new crush and his graying beard, pottery is, as Mr. Crunch would say, blowing my mind.

I could seriously type a thousand pages about pottery. It is all about clay and the earth and centering. Centering is like this: The wheel just spins and spins and spins. The key to getting the clay to shape up and make something of itself is to concentrate on keeping the clay whole and secure at the center of the wheel. I have to zone into the core of me and think of nothing but where the crux of the clay is, where my center and the center of the clay and of the wheel all come together.

There is this moment when it is all perfect and the water and slippery clay are so in unison, it's like they aren't even moving at all. And I hold my breath and *IamIamIam*. And then I screw it up or there's an air bubble or whatever, and that is what it is. And, ah. It is the most amazing thing I have ever done with my hands. So far.

The classes also remind me how unique and fearless my mother is. Which, what with all that has transpired, I had conveniently forgotten. And you know, taking the D&D money may have been the gutsiest thing she has ever done in a lifetime of doing gutsy things. Instead of keeping the fires of resentment burning at white-hot-pottery-kiln-levels the rest of my days, maybe I should give her a bit of a break. I'm a little less mad at her every day. We are taking turns glazing each other's pots. We have a few off-kilter "vessels" with daisies in them in the kitchen. I'm making a mug for Dad for his new place. Trying to, anyway. Rome wasn't built in a day.

Yesterday, a Sunday, I had to ditch what was going to be a double date with Nic and the Squirrel and Matt and me so that Mom and Dad and me could go on a family date to Millennium Park. Summer hangs on in Chicago, and it is still practically as hot as a month ago, except the nights are cool. Being all together as a family is very weird, surreal, sad, and uncomfortable. Still.

Mom didn't know what to wear. We were in her room and she was pulling clothes from her drawers like a sitcom teenager before a date with the school quarterback, which is so not what this was.

"I want to look decent but not great," she said and ended up wearing a beaded T-shirt and a denim skirt and her Crocs ballet flats, like a camp counselor on talent show night. I wore some sort of going downtown outfit but didn't obsess, though I did bring my Plathware cardigan for moral support.

I was nervous too. I didn't want them to scream about Amanda. I'm so over her already, even if they are not. I also didn't want to make awkward chitchat about the D&D, which my mom has nothing to do with now. I didn't want them to give each other longing and knowing glances fraught with meaning that only the long-married and soon-to-finalize-a-divorce would understand. I didn't want to feel like a third wheel.

There were so many ways I knew I didn't want to feel that when we finally parked in the garage beneath the park and walked over the bridge to the fountain, I was as shocked as anyone that we were all having a great time. Well, at least a good time. I mean, we just—were.

There's this fountain that is a giant four-inch deep wading pool with these two giant video screens that spit water at each other. Security there zooms around on Segways, and couples in tuxes and wedding dresses pose for wedding pictures. It's like being on the holodeck on *Star Trek*. It is otherworldly and really peaceful, unlike any other place we have been together as a family. Matt and I had always talked about going, but we never seemed to get around to it. And being there for the first time with my parents was important to me. We needed new ways to be together. What is more utopian and fresh-faced than Millennium Park?

What was most amazing was that there were protesters there. They were protesting what I thought was a war, or blood for oil, or the environmental degradation of the earth (all good candidates), but no. They were protesting *meat*. They wore cartoon animal masks, a lamb, a cow, Porky Pig with electrical tape *X*s on the eyes. One really chubby (vegan) dude in a shockingly creepy sheep mask was dancing in the center of the giant wading pool, splashing around like a maniac with a sandwich board on him that had a website on it. Happy Cow or Vegans Go dot something or other.

Since the summer, I have decided that I should start meaning what I say. To make choices and stick with them. I thought that deciding I was *not* going to sleep with Matt was going to make my life easier and less fraught, and it has. Same with my vegetarian longings. Vegan is pushing it, but the beach hot dog I shared with Dad is going to be the last morsel of dead flesh that's going to pass my lips. And I'm for real. Just say it and make it so. Besides, I love cheese.

Anyway, this X-eyed maniac was tossing flyers with the

vegan food pyramid on it, and my meat-slinging parents had no one there to impress but me, and they did. Intrigued, they took a few pamphlets and put them in their pocket/purse. I told them they should each put one on their respective refrigerators so they'd know what to feed me. After much nervous giggling, we walked over to the Bean.

Oh, the Bean.

With poetry and now ceramics, I am obsessed with forms of all kinds. "Forms" is a pretentious way of saying shapes, but is a better fit for what the Bean does to my insides. It's this giant, um, bean. Its real name is *Cloud Gate* but no one calls it that. I don't know if it's chrome or stainless steel or what, but it is globular, and its surface is mirror-shiny. It looks like it dropped out of the sky, a gift from benign and delightful aliens who expect the best from us humans. It's like the entrance to the future.

All these visitors were swarming it like ants, rushing up to laugh at their reflections, which were all swooping and elongated because of the Bean's elegant curves and dips. I went underneath and looked straight up to its center, like the underbelly of some kind of pregnant electroplated whale.

Then my parents caught up next to me and we were, right then, for that one moment, together, a family connected with an invisible magnetic pull that was intensified in the cave that the sculpture made. I knew this feeling was fleeting and hard to make stay, but it was the best thing about the three of us, and was the forever kind of love you read about. And then I looked up at the throng of people swarming the Bean in their stupid shorts and baseball caps, strollers and digital cameras, and there we were. Mom. Me. Dad. Our reflections all swirly and gloopy and totally distorted but clearly and forever:

Us.

And then Dad got a call on his cell and Mom went to read the artist statement, and I was alone—at last—with the Bean. And I thought, as any Plathian worth their salt would, of Esther Greenwood in the hospital, knocking a tray of thermometers off the bed just to piss off the nurses. Of course, my pal Esther picks up a quivering liquid metal ball of mercury, to play with. (Not that anyone could ever handle such a known carcinogen today and not get put in a decontamination chamber.)

And just by thinking it, Sylvia and me and Esther were all connected. *Cloud Gate* was a giant ball of Esther's mercury, and the way it curved over me, at once solid and invisible, was my own new kind of bell jar. In the center of it, above my head, there was a perfect reflected circle of chrome, and as I turned my face up toward the core, I couldn't remember where I was or who I was, only that my face was in the middle and my body had its own center, and blue sky and reflected clouds bounced all around me.

Everything is connected.

Nothing is what it seems.

I was shattered.

Now I am intact.

I closed my eyes, rolling them back in my head so I was fused into a whole again, and everything was paperweight sparkle and children laughing and fountains splashing and the deep metallic chime of my heart against the walls of *Cloud Gate*—

I am

I am

I sofa king am.

ACKNOWLEDGMENTS

Special thanks to my charming and tireless agent, Suzie Townsend, and all the people at Fineprint Literary Management. Respect and gratitude to Annette Pollert, the best editor I have ever had, and the supportive team at Simon Pulse. Thanks to Brenden Deneen for finding me, and Anica Mrose Rissi for liking my pages. Thanks to my fellow Plathian Peter K Steinberg at sylviaplathinfo.blogspot.com, and Emily Garber at StupidNailPolishNames.blogspot.com. Thank you to my friends and colleagues for their moral and actual support, especially Meg Mullins, Sarah Langan, Cathleen Davitt Bell, M. M. De Voe, Pen Parentis, Melissa Guion, Maribeth Batcha, and Hannah Tinti at *One Story*, and Hannah Moskowitz.

To my English teachers Ms. Carolyn Hammerschmitt, Mrs. Dianne Kirtley, Mrs. Margaret Cain, and Mr. Kevin Riberdy; I will spend the rest of my life thanking you. Margaret Mesic Nicholson, thanking you for always being my friend. Thanks to my amazing grandmothers, Josephine Tibensky and Marie Vrhel. And to my parents, Kristine

Vrhel and Robert Tibensky, thank you for everything, including my dysfunctional Czech Bohemian pirate family upbringing that made me who I am today. I love you. To Adam and Arthur for gleefully complicating my life and making it better. And to my dashing, patient, beloved, and prizewinning Scotsman, Mark Edgar, for making everything possible—thank you.

ABOUT THE AUTHOR

Arlaina Tibensky holds an MFA from Columbia University and her short fiction has appeared in *One Story*, *Inkwell*, and the *Madison Review*, among others. She curates and cohosts the acclaimed Pen Parentis Literary Salon in New York City. She lives in Manhattan with her husband and two young sons. This is her first novel. Find out more at arlainatibensky. blogspot.com.

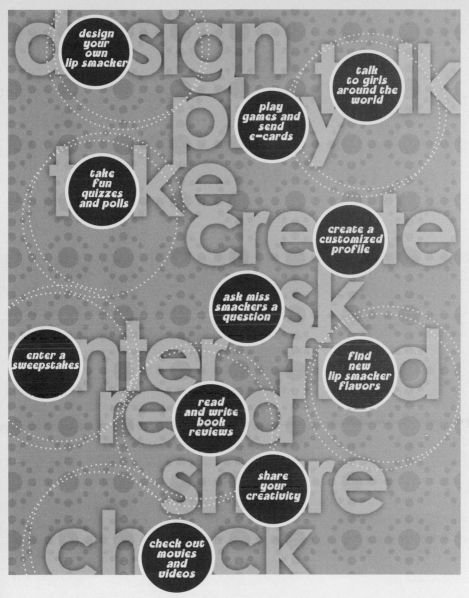

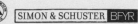

SimonTEEN

Simon & Schuster's **Simon Teen**
e-newsletter delivers current updates on
the hottest titles, exciting sweepstakes, and
exclusive content from your favorite authors.

Visit **TEEN.SimonandSchuster.com** to
sign up, post your thoughts, and find out what
every avid reader is talking about!

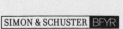